COLD WAR STORIES

Alfred Wellnitz

ISBN 13: 978-1-7348450-0-6 (paperback)

Contents

Foreword

During the Cold War period (1947 through 1991), many of the resources of the United States were devoted to Cold War activities. It wasn't a war in the normal sense. "The Cold War was a period of geopolitical tension between the Soviet Union with its satellite states (the Eastern Bloc), and the United States with its allies (the Western Bloc) after World War II." Excerpted from Wikipedia "Cold War."

"The United States adopted a foreign policy of containment of Soviet expansionism threatening strategically vital regions during the Cold War. The Cold War ended between the Revolutions of the Eastern Bloc nations in 1989 and the 1991 collapse of the USSR which ended communism in Eastern Europe. The term "cold" is used because there was no large scale fighting directly between the United States and USSR but they each supported major regional conflicts." Excerpted in part from Wikipedia "Cold War."

People who were involved in aspects of the Cold War may not have associated what they were doing with being part of the Cold War. That was true in my case. Only later in life, after the Cold War was over, did it occur to me that I had spent most of my working years involved in Cold War activities. I spent seven years in the US Navy starting in 1947, at the beginning of the Cold War, took a four-year break to earn a bachelor's degree in electrical engineering, then worked on government defense contracts for thirty-three years before retiring from engineering work at the time the Cold War was ending.

From Here and Back

Foreword

This story is about the Cold War and a reluctant B-47 crew who went through what they believed was a routine training flight that turned into a mission they had trained for but never expected to execute. The B-47 bomber was a plane that played a major role during the Cold War in the 1950s and early 1960s in United States' efforts to deter Russian aggression. The B-47 plays an important role in this story, but the detailed description of its functions and operations are not to be considered factual.

From Here and Back

I'm the only son, the only child, of Isadore and Janice Ilson. I heard my pa wanted to give me a decent Swedish name like Gottfried, but my ma insisted on naming me Erick. I'm glad she prevailed.

I would crank up the homemade tractor that my pa had cobbled together and use its power to drive a feed grinder that ground a mixture of corn and oats to feed to our chickens and pigs. I started calling the homemade tractor the Ilson. The name stuck. The Ilson featured a flathead sixty-horsepower V8 Ford motor and a car chassis with a modified transmission geared down for better traction and slower forward speed. The two back wheels were seventy-two inches apart and straddled two rows of corn spaced thirty-six inches apart. It had a single front wheel. The body of the Ilson was jacked up so a cultivator Pa had designed that fit between the front wheel and the back wheels could be used to cultivate hip-high corn.

However, today I was using the Ilson to grind grain. In order to transfer power to the grinder, a belt pulley was attached to the left rear wheel. I drove the Ilson to a well-marked spot, rolled out a belt from the granary, and attached one end of the belt to the grinder pulley. I then loosened a sort of a kickstand attached to the axle near the left wheel. I started moving the Ilson forward. The left wheel lifted off the ground, supported by the kickstand. The belt tightened, and the Ilson's left hind wheel turned freely. All the Ilson's power was transferred to the spinning wheel, turning the grinder. Grain began pouring out of two spouts from two overhead grain bins, feeding corn and oats into the grinder. After the grain mixture reached a certain level in the grinder, a prod sensor shut the spouts down until the grain fell to a certain level in the grinder, and then grain would flow again.

The processed grain fell from the bottom of the grinder onto a conveyer belt that carried it into the box of another machine Pa had cobbled together, our yard tractor. I called it the Runabout. It was also three-wheeled; the front half of a motorcycle my dad rescued from a junk yard and welded it to the back half of a car chassis. He used an extended drive chain and clever gear box to transfer power to the rear wheels.

I always considered my pa Isadore something between a tinkerer and a misplaced genius. He had immigrated here from Sweden in his teens. He was not the oldest son, so there would be no place for him on the ancestral Ilson farm, and he saw the United States as an opportunity to better his prospects. He worked as a farm hand in eastern South Dakota near Milbank and ended up marrying the farmer's daughter, Janice, my ma. They inherited the farm when they were young.

Isadore learned to read and write in Swedish and had a propensity for numbers. He picked up English quickly. He was a tinkerer, always taking things apart and finding new uses for them; eager to learn about all the new mechanical things he was seeing, either in person or in pictures. I understood he was not a particularly good farmer. He would be busy on some project, taking something apart and making it into something different, and lose track of what needed to be done on the farm.

When farmers started converting to combine use after World War II, Pa found a farmer who was moving up to a large self-propelled combine and was anxious to have someone take his small combine off his hands. It needed some work. Pa acquired it in return for fixing some problems with the farmer's tractor.

To drive its operations, the combine needed a tractor with a power take-off. But the Ilson didn't have a power take-off—or the power to use it if it had. That didn't deter Pa. He had picked up a Volkswagen air-cooled motor somewhere. He planned to use it to power the combine, mounting the motor on the combine and using the Ilson to pull the combine through the fields.

A problem with Pa's plan was that both his oats and wheat were ready to harvest when he started the project. Pa had me to swath the grain crops while he toiled over integrating the motor and the combine. The swathed grain lay in the fields for a long time. It rained. By the time he got the combine and motor working, most of the grain had spoiled. I didn't say anything about it—neither did Ma. We both knew Pa's urge to tinker was incurable.

I was amazed by some of the things Pa came up with—not that they worked well or worked better than anything already out there but rather that they worked at all. Though I do have to admit that he had more successes than outright failures.

I went to the Milbank high school. At the time, most farm kids didn't go to high school. Not that those parents were against education. It was expensive. There was no busing for farm kids. Farmers were recovering from the Great Depression and an historic drought. During World War II they were making money, finally, but they had a lot of catching up to do. However, both Pa and Ma were big fans of education. You wouldn't think Pa would think like that since he had only spent four years inside a schoolroom, but I think he was even more set on me going to high school than Ma was.

I used the Runabout to commute. Licensing wasn't a big issue in South Dakota at the time, and the Runabout had no trouble keeping up with traffic. In addition, Pa fashioned a cab for the rider and made it cozy in the winter. Another benefit was that I would deliver the ten-gallon milk cans to the small cheese factory in Milbank before classes started. Pa hated the cows, but they provided the steady income our family needed.

I did okay in high school, especially math. My math teacher, Miss Schwandt, said I should continue my education, go to college. Ma and Pa appreciated my grades but didn't mention college—for a good reason. Our family didn't have the means to send me to college. Farmers had done well during the war and since, but Pa really wasn't a farmer; he was a tinkerer. In the best of times, we just got by.

Miss Schwandt wasn't ready to concede. She came up with an idea. "At Brookings they have ROTC. If you qualify you could have most of your expenses paid. I can get the forms you need."

By Brookings, she meant the town where South Dakota State College was, sixty miles south of Milbank. It was a popular college for students from the Milbank area. I knew they had an engineering major, which was what I would want, so the idea appealed to me. I thought it was nice of Miss Schwandt to want to help me, and I told her so. I said that I would appreciate her obtaining the forms.

When I got the forms, I discovered there were both army and air force ROTCs at Brookings. I talked to my folks about the idea. Ma was in favor of it right away. Pa seemed a little hesitant. I suppose he was hoping I would help on the farm after high school. If I was around to do the farming work, he would have more time to tinker. I had thought about that. What was my long-term goal? Did I have one? I pretty much understood that I could partner with Pa. If I really wanted to be a farmer that might not be a bad idea. I would pretty much have a free hand to do what I wanted with farming if Pa was left to his tinkering. Did I want to be a farmer? That was a question I hadn't figured out the answer to.

Pa listened without comment when I told them about the ROTC option. "It's not a sure thing," I explained. "Not everyone who applies is accepted, and there is a physical." Ma was sure I would be accepted and left no doubt that she thought I should go for it. Finally, Pa opened with a little cough. "Erick," he said, "if I had da chance you got, I vould yomp all over it. Can't get too much education. Dat much I know."

Which would be the best to apply for, army or air force? In the army, they mostly shot people. In the air force, they flew airplanes. The idea of flying airplanes seemed to fit in with studying engineering better than shooting people. I filled out the application for the air force ROTC.

I received the acceptance before it was time to register for the fall quarter at South Dakota State. The physical was administered by our regular family doctor and was kind of a joke. The doctor said the main thing was to see if you were too fat. "Your real physical will happen when you go on active duty."

I decided I would work for a degree in mechanical engineering, somewhat related to what Pa did when he tinkered, which I could relate to because Pa had me help sometimes, especially when he needed to move heavy things like car motors from one place to another.

I found myself studying harder than I had ever studied before. I received As in my math courses, but I had to work hard to get them. Fortunately, the extra classes I had to take for ROTC were easy, and the physical training and activity involved were good; otherwise I would likely have been going downhill in those categories. In the summer we took two weeks of training at an air force facility to become familiar with some of the things the air force was doing. Upon graduating in June 1961, I was commissioned as a second lieutenant in the United States Air Force. My orders directed me to report to Offutt Air Force Base near Omaha, Nebraska.

At Offutt I underwent a genuine physical checkup. I guess the physical determined what kinds of things you would be able to do in the air force. If I got into something involving engineering, I would be happy.

After the physical and a bunch of written tests, I was interviewed and then informed of what I was qualified to do. Physically, I was qualified to take pilot training; I was encouraged to go in that direction. I also learned that pilot training was like signing up for a career. Most other skill paths required only two years of active duty and two years in the reserves. Pilot training could require more than two years, so you were obligated to serve more active time. I told the interviewer I wasn't interested in being a pilot or having a career in the air force. I would prefer to do engineering work with a contractor or in a lab, something like that.

The interviewer seemed surprised. He said most people he interviewed would give their left arm to be a pilot. He went on; they were looking for more than pilots to be airmen. The active-duty requirements for most nonpilot airmen required only two years of active duty.

"We are looking for men like yourself to man large numbers of SAC aircraft coming off the line," the interviewer said.

He almost made it sound like it would be my patriotic duty to do this. The interviewer described a position as a navigator/bombardier on a B-47 and encouraged me to consider it. "As a navigator/bombardier on a B-47, you would only have a two-year active-duty obligation, and you would also receive flight pay."

The interviewer showed me pictures of the B-47. In one picture the plane was sitting in a flight line, and in another it was in flight. I'd heard about the B-47 but knew little about the plane. The idea that I would be riding in one of them sharpened my interest. I studied the pictures. In the air, it was a beautiful-looking flying machine, a big fighter plane with six jet engines. In another way, it appeared ominous to me, like something evil. However, I was a farm boy, always wanting to please, so I relented and agreed to take the training to be the navigator on a B-47.

Soon, it seemed I was in a world of quick time. I was ordered to report to the Mather Air Force Base, near Sacramento, California. Six months later I was deemed able to perform the duties of a B-47 navigator/bombardier and ordered back to Offutt Field. I was assigned to a wing stationed there.

After completing navigation training, I saw my first real-life B-47 at Offutt. It was more imposing than in the photos. It looked unlike anything I had ever seen before, with swept-back wings that drooped when the jet was parked and flexed up seventeen feet at the wing tips when airborne. It was a fearsome-looking, delicate flying machine designed to fly higher and faster than anything that would oppose it in the air, high enough to be safe from ground-based weapons. It was developed to penetrate Russian airspace and deliver nuclear bombs to selected targets. Those goals, faster and higher than Russian fighters and beyond the range of ground-based weapons, took priority over durability, crew comfort, survivability, and everything else.

B47 Design Featured Major Advances in Aircraft Technology

Photo available for use without restrictions

There were only three crew members, pilot, co-pilot and navigator—a departure from World War II, when heavy bombers often had nine or more crew members. Part of the reason for a smaller crew was the lack of armament. The B-47 had two fifty-caliber machine guns in the tail, which were operated remotely by the co-pilot. The B-47 depended on flying high and being fast in order to reach targets. Each member of the small crew was responsible for tasks that would have been shared with other crewmen in previous large bomber designs.

The pilot and co-pilot sat under a bubble-type canopy. They had a good view of the surroundings, but the space was cramped, reminiscent of a fighter plane cockpit. My accommodations in the nose cone were more ample, but there were no windows. I had a viewing screen that could monitor the outside world, but that was not the same as an unrestricted view.

Not that I needed to look out a window to navigate, but it would have been nice.

One thing that unnerved me at first was that, in case of a bailout, the navigator would be ejected down, not up. This required that the plane be at an altitude of at least five hundred feet before a downward ejection would work. Worse yet, in practice, the downward ejection seemed to have problems at any altitude. After a while I got over worrying about it because I figured I would never have a reason to eject from the plane. That might have been illogical thinking, but it worked.

Each crew was a team and would remain a team of three until some event like retirement from active duty or reassignment brought a change. The crews tended to be young, mostly first and second lieutenants. The pilot on our plane was First Lieutenant Richard Douglas. He loved flying and the air force and planned to make a career out of it. He was young, not much older than I was, and this was his first aircraft. He thought he was the luckiest man alive to get to fly the B-47. Second Lieutenant Bill VanVeen was the co-pilot, waiting to complete his air force active duty commitment so he could fly commercial, although the B-47 was not an ideal aircraft for commercial training because it was so different. I hoped his plans would work for him.

When I reported for duty, a second lieutenant navigator/bombardier, in the spring of 1961, the Strategic Air Force was on a high alert. Planes were loaded and ready to take off on a mission to attack Russia.

Every third week, the crews in the section I was assigned to, spent the week in a building near where our plane sat on a hardstand. Three crews shared the building, which had everything needed to accommodate nine crew members for the week. A contractor supplied people to cook meals, wash clothes, make beds, and clean. The crew members underwent training and information sessions. We'd fly one long mission during the week. Otherwise we could do pretty much what we wanted except leave the building or immediate area. I started reading. I read more books than ever before. There was an exercise room, plus a hobby room with woodworking, ceramics, painting, and metalworking where I messed around.

During the week, our section of three planes would fly a mission. Soon after being alerted to take off, the crews sprinted to their planes, which were being run up by ground crew members. Our three-man crew hardly had time to settle into our positions before we joined a line of nine planes moving toward the runway, fully loaded with fuel and nuclear weapons. There was no hesitation, no calling the tower for permission to take off. When the first plane in the line reached the takeoff point on the runway, it immediately started its takeoff run and, with the assistance of JATO (jet assisted take-off) rockets, was soon airborne. The following eight B-47s lined up and took off at sixteen-second intervals after the first plane. My plane was in the middle of the pack. That meant we took off in the wake of the plane ahead of us and had to deal with a lot of turbulence.

The missions normally included refueling over Alaska or north of Greenland. We were to consider every mission a for-real mission to bomb some Russian target. We carried sealed orders onboard to be opened once we crossed a point of no return. If we weren't recalled and ordered back to base before we reached the point of no return, we knew that we were on a real mission, with orders to bomb a designated target. We never had to open those orders and never expected to open them.

When not on alert, we received extended time off to make up for the one-week confinement in alert quarters, and after that we participated in training exercises and honed our job skills.

Things had changed since the B-47 was introduced to the air force in 1951. Russia had developed a fighter plane and a ground missile that could reach the B-47 when it flew at its service ceiling. So, we were trained to fly low instead of high to limit radar detection and to use a variable track in place of a straight-in approach to the target. When the target area was reached, the plane would regain enough altitude to allow the nuclear weapon to detonate at its intended altitude and for the plane to escape being blown up. The need for a zig-zag approach and terrain-avoidance maneuvers put a strain on the aircraft and on the pilot and navigator. The changes also affected fuel consumption. Flying at a low altitude burned three times as much fuel as flying at the service altitude of thirty-five thousand to forty thousand feet.

In October 1962, we started hearing that Russia was establishing missile launch sites in Cuba. Airmen I associated with didn't get too excited about this news. We were always hearing about the Russians doing this or that, and this sounded like another one of those Cold War stories that came up and then faded away.

However, this time seemed different. Soon after we heard about the missile launch sites, the whole wing at Offutt went to alert status; everyone was confined to the base until further notice. All the aircraft rated ready to fly were loaded with nuclear weapons. Our three-plane section received orders to be ready to take off at three a.m. on October twenty-second. That was unusual. Normally there would be no warning. The klaxon would go off, and we would race to get to the airplane and take off as fast as we could, like firemen responding to a fire.

Our three-plane section joined six other aircraft and took off as scheduled at three a.m., headed north. Normally we would head for Alaska or Greenland, where we would rendezvous with tankers to refuel. However, this time we were to fly almost straight north over Canadian territory, across the North Pole, and then head south toward Russia before refueling.

Navigating the leg from Offutt to the refueling destination wasn't much of a challenge. I had LORAN (long range navigation), radio direction finders, a gyro compass, and unlimited use of radar.

The crew was supplied with two C rations each and a thermos of coffee. On this mission, the first C ration was breakfast. I usually didn't eat the second ration, but if I did it would be during the return to Offutt. There was very little variety in the C rations; if you ate one you knew what to expect.

Refueling was always an exciting part of a mission. No matter how many times we did it, it never became routine. We'd fly a little lower and behind the tanker using the flying boom method. A combination of lights and verbal communication between the tanker boom operator and our pilot put us in position for the flying probe to mate with our plane's refueling coupling. During the refueling, our plane had to maintain a position that maintained the probe connection. Two planes flying hundreds of miles an hour, connected by a fueling probe, with restricted freedom to maneuver, can cause anxiety. Particularly in the Arctic region, where spending much time considering bailing out was an exercise in futility—the possibility of survival was unlikely. Fortunately, once the connection was made, it didn't take long to complete the refueling.

Once the refueling was complete on that October 1962 flight, we continued on course to complete the mission. I waited for the recall that always occurred before we reached the point of no return. It bothered me a little that we weren't very far from Russia when we'd refueled and that we didn't have much time before a recall would become irrelevant.

Richard, the pilot, was also getting nervous. His voice came over the intercom. "How far to point of no return?"

"Twenty minutes," I replied.

Bill, the co-pilot, chimed in. "This story isn't following the script."

The pilot agreed. "I have no desire to visit Russia this time of the year."

"Ten minutes to go," I said.

"We could abort, engine problem," the co-pilot suggested.

"Everything is purring," the pilot replied.

"I know, just suggesting," the co-pilot replied. "Or just hoping."

"Five minutes," I said.

At this point I realized that what would never happen was about to happen. School children were being taught what to do when this thing that would never happen, happened. People had become used to the idea that a nuclear war would likely be the end of human existence, but they also knew it would never happen. But as this crew in this B-47 passed through the point of no return, we knew it was about to happen.

"Okay," I said, "we've passed the point of no return. Time to check out our itinerary." I had a package, and the pilot had an identical package. It identified the target, the route to the target, and the procedure for flying the route to the target before releasing the device. The target was Moscow. We were being directed to end life on earth as we knew it. Strange how my mind focused on how we would accomplish this.

It would be up to our crew to follow the package directions and complete the mission. Everything was in our hands and our B-47, a dot in the sky that could destroy a city. We would be flying low in order to minimize detection by Russian radar. My first task would be to navigate the course to the target—no small task when flying low on a zig-zag course at night with only a gyro compass. We would be running silent. No radar, no radio transmissions, no running lights.

The pilot noted that the forecast was for a clear sky when we reached the Russian coastline.

"I appreciate the help," I replied. "With a nearly full moon we will be able to navigate visually. There are some low mountains along the coast we will want to avoid"

"Roger that." The pilot replied.

As forecast, the sky was clear when we reached the Russian coastline, with a forecast for partial clouds two hundred miles in and rain and light drizzle over Moscow. We would reach Moscow at midnight.

We were flying at thirty-five thousand feet but dropped to five hundred feet as we entered the Barents Sea and approached the Russian mainland, where an estuary linked the Barents and White Seas about a hundred miles east of Murmansk. As predicted, there was a nearly full moon, and we could visually navigate the narrow body of water connecting the Barents and White Seas.

"Man!" I exclaimed. "I don't know how you could navigate through there with instruments!"

The co-pilot agreed. "Some of those hills on either side of that water are taller than five hundred feet by quite a bit."

The White Sea was a relatively small body of water, but it provided a path through the low mountain range near the coast to the flat terrain along its southern shore. We had been told that snoops continually searched for and identified cracks in Russian border radar coverage; it seemed to work for us. We had easily penetrated Russian territory. Considering the immensity of the Union of Soviet Socialist Republics (USSR), it seemed likely there could be holes in the border security.

We maintained our five-hundred-foot altitude over the flat, dark terrain south of the White Sea. We tracked southwesterly after leaving the White Sea, which pointed us toward Leningrad. We occasionally saw flickering lights but no massed lights like those visible above a village or city. Although it was dark, it was obvious that we were flying over a lightly inhabited forest.

No swarms of MiG fighters rose to intercept us. We seemed to move through Russian air space alone and unnoticed. There had to be other SAC bombers attacking, but everything seemed peaceful and quiet.

We were flying under scattered clouds when we reached the coordinates to change our heading to a southeasterly direction. Those coordinates were based on my best estimates of wind direction and velocity, the accuracy of our gyro compass, and not much else. It would have been nice to have a firm fix on our position before making the turn, but it was not necessary. Finding a bright, shiny target as large as Moscow shouldn't be difficult.

Our track ran parallel to and about sixty miles to the east of a busy highway that connected Leningrad and Moscow. The terrain remained flat, ideal for low altitude flight. I gave the mission planners a good grade for selecting ideal conditions for a terrain-hugging track.

We saw more scattered lights and the glow of numerous lights from villages and small towns. We flew low, without running lights, so people might think we were a ghost ship in the sky when we flashed by. Still no obvious defensive activity. This seemed easier than it should be.

We encountered light rain and mist, which would make our approach to Moscow more difficult to detect. I alerted the crew to the next course change, which would happen in twenty minutes, at 2245 Greenwich meantime. We would then turn ninety degrees to a heading that would put us south of Moscow in fifteen minutes. After the turn, we made another turn, climbing to thirty thousand feet on a heading that put us over Moscow. As we climbed, the co-pilot and I turned on interlocking switches to arm the nuclear device. When the sequence was successful, a red "ready" light lit up on both my and the co-pilot's panels. Only two things remained in order to complete the final arming of the nuclear device. First, when the weapon dropped out of the bomb bay, a sensor in the nose cone would determine that the weapon was clear of the aircraft and falling freely. Reaching a specified altitude above the surface was the last step necessary to allow detonation. The nuclear device in the bomb bay was set to detonate at one thousand feet above Moscow.

The cloud cover provided no protection against the intense light and gamma rays that would be emitted when the weapon exploded. I pulled on my eye-protection goggles. All this seemed completely surreal.

We were high above the cloud cover when we reached thirty thousand feet. Moscow could be seen as a pale glow of light through the clouds, a big bullseye—adequate since close is good enough with nuclear devices. We passed over Moscow, then made a hundred-and-eighty-degree turn. I opened the bomb bay doors and released the bomb. It should fall approximately in the middle of Moscow. I didn't feel the lift normally experienced when an item weighing 7,600 pounds was dropped from a plane.

Neither did the pilot. His voice came over the intercom. "What happened? I didn't feel a release."

I looked at my panel. The bomb-bay-door-open light was on. The bomb bay door should have closed after the device was released. "Something is wrong," I answered. "Looks like the weapon didn't release."

I felt a tremendous load lift off my shoulders. We had followed our orders and carried them out successfully—until the moment the bomb didn't release. Hundreds of thousands of humans were still alive.

If there is a God, I thought, *thank you*.

"What the hell!" the pilot exclaimed. "We have a hot nuke on board."

The co-pilot asked, "What's the plan?"

The plane continued following the heading it had been on for releasing the weapon. That was okay, since that is what was planned—however, not with the weapon still in the bomb bay. We had not experienced the bright light emitted when a weapon detonates nor been buffeted by shock waves, further evidence that something was amiss.

There was a long pause after the co-pilot's question. I thought, *What would my pa do?* This was Pa's kind of problem, and he would have a solution he could implement with the tools he had. From my weapon control panel, I attempted to set the altitude at which the nuclear weapon would activate to a lower altitude, but it didn't respond.

Flight crews had been briefed on the things we should know about the weapon. One item that stuck in my mind from the briefings was that one of the last activation requirements was for a sensor in the nose cone to sense that the device was free of the aircraft and falling free. I told the pilot to drop us down to five thousand feet and gave him a new heading.

The pilot asked, "Heading to where? What about the locked and loaded nuke in the bomb bay?"

"We'll have to take care of the problem in our bomb bay on the way to Incirlik Air Base in Turkey. We'll drop down to five thousand feet so we don't have to keep the cabin pressurized while we work on our problem, but not so low that the weapon could be activated. Anybody have a Swiss Army knife?" I asked.

The co-pilot replied, "Wouldn't ever leave the house without one. Why?"

"Throw it down here," I replied. I didn't know what I would do with the knife, but I wanted to make it seem like I had a plan.

I observed on my nav panel altimeter that the pilot had begun dropping down from thirty thousand feet. I could start trying to break into the bomb bay without worrying about cabin pressure when or if I could do it.

I looked around my space. The bombsight was mounted next to the navigator's table. I noticed it was on a base consisting of two aluminum bars about a foot long, four inches wide, and half an inch thick. Phillips head screws attached the bombsight to the aluminum bars, and the bars were fastened to the plane deck with more Phillips head screws. The Swiss Army knife had a Phillips head screwdriver in its repertoire, but that seemed like a lot of screws for the fragile Swiss Army knife to handle. The bombsight was raised on a pedestal about a foot and a half high. Without giving it too much thought, I sat down on the plane deck, braced my feet against the navigation table, put my arms around the bombsight, and leaned back. One of the aluminum bars attached to the bombsight pulled loose; the other stayed attached to the plane deck but detached from the bombsight. The screws attached to the deck and to the bombsight had been loosened and could be removed using the Swiss Army knife. Soon I had two heavy pieces of metal to work with.

I used one bar as a wedge and the other as a hammer. I placed the end of the wedge bar next to a row of rivets and began pounding on it with the other bar.

When I started pounding, the pilot shouted, "What in hell are you doing? Are you destroying the aircraft?"

I explained that I was trying to break a hole in the bulkhead to get a look at the weapon, and then I resumed pounding. Finally, a small crack opened in the bulkhead. Working on the small crack with the wedge bar, I opened a hole large enough to push the wedge bar into. I then used the wedge bar as a lever to peel back the aluminum far enough to put my arm through. I was able to see into the bomb bay.

Using flashlight that was attached my life jacket, I observed that the weapon's tail end hung loose; the front end remained firmly held by its hanger. The hanging tail kept the bomb bay doors from closing.

I described what I saw to the pilot.

"How stable does the situation look?" he asked.

"Hard to tell," I replied. "If the nuke doesn't fall free before I can reach it with one of my bars and smash the sensor in the cone, it will be safe." I was assuming that in the process of smashing the cone, I wouldn't accidently activate the weapon. I assumed that it required a positive signal to activate, that it would not activate if it received no signal.

I reported, "I can reach the cone with my bar." A short time later I reported that I had smashed the cone with my bar. "Okay," I said, "drop down to radar-avoiding altitude, five hundred feet."

This would be the real test to determine if my assumption about the sensor was valid. We dropped below a thousand feet and we didn't blow up. In one of my engineering classes, the professor had said that when you assume, you make an ass out of you and me. The professor was proved wrong in this case.

We were soon skimming over the Ukraine's flat terrain with few obstacles, cruising at five hundred feet. It continued to puzzle me why, after we had flown thousands of miles through Russian airspace, there was no response from Soviet defense forces. I mentioned this to the crew.

"Suits me," the co-pilot answered. "I had considered bombing Russia a suicide mission."

"It is," I answered. "Assuming other planes are successful."

The pilot agreed. "Everything seems so quiet and peaceful—this isn't the way it's supposed to go."

"Peace on earth, good will to all," the co-pilot replied.

We reached the Black Sea and continued flying at five hundred feet above the water until we reached a point where we felt it was safe to climb to 10,000 feet.

The pilot asked about the fuel situation. Could we reach Incirlik? The co-pilot monitored the fuel and asked me how far it was to Incirlik. I had established a good fix on our position when we reached the Black Sea and gave him a number I had high confidence in.

"Okay," the co-pilot said. "Hang on while I run the numbers." After a long pause the co-pilot reported his conclusion. "Based on flying at our current altitude and assuming wind isn't a factor, we need to refuel before we reach Incirlik."

"Ok," The pilot said, "See if you can raise Incirlik about getting a tanker to refule."

The co-pilot handled the communications. He received no response to his calls on air force frequencies. He tried Turkish airways. Same result.

He called me on the intercom. "Nav, could you look at our radios? We should be able to communicate with somebody. I'm not getting anyone. Something must be wrong."

I had a reputation as the fix-it guy in our crew. I could usually resolve problems or figure out a way to work around them. Must have inherited some of Pa's tinkering ways.

The communications equipment rack was in an unpressurized portion of the plane, accessible through a removable access cover that put the plane's transmitters and receivers within reach. I gained access to the communications equipment and started working on the problem.

I asked the co-pilot to transmit something. There was a power output indicator on the front of the transmitter, and it indicated a strong signal as the co-pilot transmitted. Two receivers provided dual redundancy. One receiver had an obvious problem. It was cold, without power, but the other one had power. A phone jack allowed direct connection to each receiver. I plugged my earphones into the receiver with power. A functional receiver would have background noise; this one did not. Back to the other receiver. I found an obvious problem; a circuit breaker had been tripped. I reset the circuit breaker and heard background noise. So much for dual redundancy. Both receivers had been down for different reasons.

I called up the co-pilot on the intercom. "Okay, you should be able to communicate."

The co-pilot communicated with the Incirlik Air Force Base and identified our plane. The pilot and I were monitoring the conversation. There seemed to be some confusion at the other end. Then a voice requested our plane's identification and asked for the origin of the flight. Then it asked for the names of the crewmen.

The co-pilot supplied the information and added that we had a hung nuclear device in the plane.

There was a long pause in the communications and the pilot came on the intercom. "Do you think?"

I replied, "I do. Maybe we were recalled and never received the message."

"Damn," the pilot replied.

About this time two F-86 fighter planes appeared on our wing, looking us over.

Incirlik finally came back and requested more information.

The co-pilot described the nuclear device hang-up and said that we couldn't close the bomb bay because one end of the device hung down, preventing its closing.

There was another long pause before the voice said the plane could not land at Incirlik with a nuclear device hanging out of the bomb bay.

As we approached the northern coast of Turkey, Turkish airways asked for information. Incirlik interceded and got us cleared for an overfly.

The co-pilot informed Incirlik of the other problem that put the hung-up nuclear device in second place. "We are short of fuel and need to be refueled in order to reach Incirlik."

This was a problem Incirlik could handle, and they got right back. "We have a loaded tanker that will take off shortly to intercept and refuel your plane."

That settled, they returned to the puzzle of the hung-up nuclear device. The co-pilot assured Incirlik that the weapon was safe.

A long pause followed before Incirlik came back with directions. They instructed us to drop the nuclear weapon off the coast in shallow Mediterranean waters.

The co-pilot sounded exasperated. "We can't drop it. It is hung up." The voice said there were two options: drop the weapon near the shore or ditch the plane in the Mediterranean near the shore.

As we were refueling, I realized I hadn't eaten the second C ration. We had been flying for twenty hours and I wasn't hungry or tired. We had been surviving on adrenaline for a long time.

It also occurred to me that I was a long way from the farm in South Dakota, in a different world I couldn't talk about and probably wouldn't want to talk about. *Strange,* I thought. *Things happen in one's life which you don't expect, don't plan for, are not prepared for, but you go along with whatever it is, like pulling a lever to release a nuclear weapon that would have killed hundreds of thousands of people but for the grace of God, who caused it to hang up. Humans can pull that lever as if it were a normal part of a job. I'm capable of doing that. Why? How?*

After we finished refueling, the pilot announced that we would try to shake our hung-up nuke loose when we reached the Mediterranean. If that wasn't successful, we should ditch the plane, again near the shore. The first alternative seemed preferable.

The pilot said we would do the "pull up, drop bomb" maneuver, something the air force had determined should not be done with the B-47 because of the strain on its fragile wings. In the maneuver, the plane makes a low approach to the target, then pulls up steeply and releases the bomb in the presence of strong gravitational forces that would eject the bomb clear of the aircraft. It might work—if the plane didn't fall apart.

We made a fast descent to near sea level, picked up a lot of airspeed, and then pulled back sharply. We shot up, pulling a lot of Gs. If that didn't break the nuke loose, nothing would.

Suddenly the plane began to roll. The pilot screamed into the intercom, "Bail out! We've lost a wing!"

I had no choice but to use the unreliable downward ejecting system. I didn't hesitate, just pulled the lever and found myself thrown from the spinning aircraft. We were above a thousand feet when the plane broke apart, plenty of time for my chute to open before I hit the water. I saw two other chutes floating down. We all hit the water at about the same time. I inflated my life jacket and untangled myself from my chute by the time I was picked up by one of several boats that had been dispatched to the area to respond to whatever happened. While the crew was being picked up, parts of our plane could be seen splashing down a few miles downrange from where we were. Very likely the nuclear device ended up somewhere near where Incirlik wanted it, but I didn't expect the crew would be receiving any mission-completed citations.

It took about half an hour for the boat to take us to a landing, where an ambulance met us. By then, I was feeling the effects of not sleeping for twenty-four hours, eating only one C ration during that time, and spending more than twenty of those hours flying under stressful conditions. Dry clothes, a meal, and a bed were at the top of my to-do list. It was not to be. We showered and were found to be tired but healthy by the medics. We received clean uniforms, and then we were interviewed by three worried-looking air force officers. Yes, we had flown across the full width of Russia and were only prevented from nuking Moscow by a malfunctioning bomb release. We had followed air force procedures. We were not recalled from the mission, so we'd opened our onboard sealed orders and proceeded to carry out those orders. And yes, we'd determined that neither of the redundant receivers were functioning when we tried to contact Incirlik Air Force Base.

After completing the interview, one of the officers, a colonel, reminded us that we all had top secret clearances and confirmed we were aware that we would not divulge information about our missions to anyone unauthorized to know about them, particularly this mission we had just completed.

It seems that two counter-balancing failures had probably prevented an all-out nuclear war from occurring.

As far as I know, the Russians may never have known about the almost-nuking of Moscow. If they had, they may have suppressed the information, not wanting to admit to the Russian people that a US military aircraft had penetrated Russian airspace and flown undetected across the breadth of the country.

I returned to Pa's farm after completing my active-duty obligation. We built a state-of-the-art machine shop and started a company called Original Design. We did custom design work, mostly for agricultural machine manufacturers but also for the auto industry. We didn't do manufacturing but did provide prototypes and proofing and testing of concepts. We trained some South Dakota farm kids to be the skilled mechanical craftsmen who built and tested our prototypes. As we incorporated electrical and electronic features into our designs, we also hired an electrical engineer and a couple of technicians. I introduced Pa to the concept of patents, and we hired a lawyer who spent most of his time researching, filing, and protecting patents we generated.

I never talked to anyone about the missions I flew in the air force, especially not about the time my crew overflew Russia because of a receiver failure and would have dropped a nuclear bomb on Moscow except that another failure caused the bomb to hang up. I look around our neighborhood, which has not changed much during my entire life, and think, *Thank God for failures.*

U.S. Naval Air
Routine Patrol

Picture by R.A. Scholefield

Prologue

This short story, "US Naval Air: Routine Patrol," although fictional, is a rendition of a number of interesting experiences actually encountered by flight crews during Electronic Reconnaissance patrol flights along the Asian coast from Vladivostok to Saigon during a two-year period between 1951 and 1953. The author flew as a crewman on the P4M-1Q planes utilized for this mission. He completed ninety-five patrols. Patrol flights originated from the Sangley Point Naval Air Station in the Philippines, the Naha Naval Air Station and Kadena Air Base in Okinawa, and the Atsugi and Iwakuni Naval Air Stations in Japan. The original members of the flight crews who volunteered for the special mission did not know what the mission would be except that it would be overseas, and they were obligated to two years of service. Once accepted, they were cleared for access to top secret information and were not allowed to divulge information about this activity until fifty years later.

U.S. Naval Air Routine Patrol

Sangley Point Naval Air Station

The crew scheduled to take off from the Sangley Point Naval Air Station at 2200 that night each packed a bag since they would end the patrol at the Kadena Air Force base in Okinawa. They would then fly an out-and-back patrol from Kadena along the China coast north of Shanghai and back along the west coast of Korea before returning to Sangley Point on a third patrol.

The enlisted flight crew made their way on foot through the dark night to the flight line located less than half a mile from their Quonset hut. Wellman, 1st radio, with MacBee, 2nd radio walked together. They had become good friends and spent many of their liberty hours together during the year the crews trained and prepared for the overseas assignment. It included attending classes on the new equipment they would be using and maintaining and picking up a still new smelling P4M-1Q aircraft retrofitted for the Electronic Counter Measure (ECM) mission at the Glenn L Martin Aircraft factory located in Baltimore Maryland.

The aircraft used for the airborne electronic surveillance mission was designated as a P4M-1Q. The "1Q" indicated that the plane had been configured for Electronic Counter Measure (ECM) operations. The P4M featured a compromise design with two conventional reciprocating engines provided the long-range capability needed in a patrol aircraft and two jet engines which could deliver speed if the plane was attacked or provide backup power during takeoff and landings or emergency. The conventional engines, two Pratt & Whitney 4360s, were the most powerful reciprocating engines ever put into use by the United States armed forces. The jets were J33 turbo jets. The plane had been designed to fight if necessary with gun turrets placed topside, fore, and aft. Nine officers and enlisted men made up a normal P4M crew, but the personnel on board grew to fourteen for ECM missions.

A total of eight P4M-1Q planes were initially assigned to the program. Four planes would be sent to North Africa to patrol areas in Europe and four sent to Sangley Point in the Philippines to patrol areas in the Far East. The four planes assigned to the Philippines were flown from the Martin factory in Baltimore to Miramar Naval Air Station near San Diego California where the crew and ground personnel spent several months getting acquainted in using and maintaining the new planes and equipment. Finally the four plane contingent was ready to deploy and took a roundabout northern route to Sangley Naval Air Station in the Philippines. The roundabout route included stops at Whidbey Island Naval Air Station near Seattle where the crews spent several days practicing Ground Control Approach (GCA) landings. The four planes then hopped to the Kodiak Naval Air Station in Alaska followed by another stop at the Shemya Airforce Base at the end of the Aleutian Chain. The final stop along the way was made at the Atsugi Navy Air Station in Japan where the flight crews were briefed on what the P4M-1Q mission would be. They were also given a scary briefing by a survival expert on what to expect and do if caught behind enemy lines. Wellman and probably most of the crewmen were thinking, *"Interesting but this won't be happening to me."*

MacBee, the older of the two, had been in the navy reserves and was called back into active duty when the Korean War started in 1950. Wellman's enlistment would have ended in 1950 if the Korean War hadn't come along. He was given the choice of having his current enlistment extended or reenlisting. If he reenlisted, he would be paid a two-hundred-dollar bonus. Wellman considered that a no-brainer and reenlisted.

He had bought a 12-gauge Remington semi-automatic shotgun with the bonus and used it to hunt quail in California.

Wellman and MacBee greeted the Special Project member who had drawn guard duty when they reached the three aircraft parked on the hardstand that night. There were four planes in the Special Project contingent, but one of the planes had flown a patrol to Japan and would be gone for a week, temporarily flying patrols from that location.

The man on guard duty worked as an aviation mechanic during the day. "Glad to see you guys," he said. "Not much going on otherwise." The guard carried a sidearm and a sawed-off 12-gauge Winchester pump shotgun. The guard was notorious because he had carried his shotgun into the enlisted club to buy a drink on New Year's Eve.

The squadron posted its own guards, the idea being to keep anyone not in the Special Project from knowing what the Special Project was about. Good luck with that. People around the base started calling the Special Project team the "fifty footers." If you got closer than fifty feet of the aircraft, they'd shoot you.

Wellman noticed they had a new bureau six digit number painted on their plane's tail. These were big numbers that could be seen from another aircraft or even from the ground when flying low. Every month a new fictitious number would be painted on the tail. Apparently this was supposed to confuse the people they were spying on. Wellman doubted if it confused anyone and was a waste of paint.

The crewmen all stopped at a Quonset hut office where a yeoman was distributing survival gear. They each received a 38-caliber revolver and a bag of survival goodies.

MacBee mumbled something about the need to carry the heavy revolver. "I couldn't hit the side of a barn with it if my life depended on it."

Johnson, the ordnance man on their crew, explained, "That's to shoot yourself if all else fails."

"Oh," MacBee replied. "You must have a different instruction book than I have."

Johnson was enjoying bringing MacBee up to date. "You must have an outdated revision, better get the latest version or you could get in trouble for not following the rules, particularly about shooting yourself."

Johnson was a lifer, a World War II vet not looking for another job. Balding, of average height, with a sparse frame, he was reliable, knew his job.

Wellman checked out the contents of his survival bag before signing it out. Some of the items in the bag made more sense than the revolver. These included a small piece of gold bullion. Always welcome everywhere. Probably the most valuable item in the package would be the waterproof parchment with a message in several different languages that said it would pay the holder ten thousand American dollars if the holder delivered the parchment along with a live American airman. Other miscellaneous items included a tube of morphine, a pocket knife, and a mirror.

The yeoman handed Johnson a small mailbag. "Some mail for the Okinawa contingent " he said. Patrol flights terminating at Okinawa normally carried any mail addressed to members of a temporarily assigned Okinawa Special Project contingent. Johnson took the bag, "The only reason those malcontents would want to see us," he replied.

After picking up their survival kits, the crew went out to the flight line to prepare the plane for the night's mission. Their plane sat first in the line-up of the three on the hardstand.

P4M-1Q

Author photograph

Sharman, the plane captain, and a member of the ground crew hooked up the auxiliary power unit, and the onboard equipment came alive. Sharman had a stocky build and seldom smiled. He knew his business and had the respect of the rest of the crew. Like most plane captains, his skill rating included aviation mechanic. He knew the plane's physical condition better than anyone, including the pilots. He, like Johnson, was a lifer, and the two of them hung out together.

Two crew members, Scarma, mechanic, and Bailey, radar man, pulled the props through a cycle. Scarma and Bailey were the youngest crew members. Bailey, blond crew cut, with eyes that always looked surprised, was a technical whiz who had two years of college and couldn't wait to get out of the service so he could finish school. Scarma was the opposite, probably a lifer, competent, down to earth.

A jeep pulled up, and Wellman helped Johnson unload boxes of rations for the flight.

"Hey, what're we going to eat tonight?" Sharman asked Johnson.

Johnson, in addition to his usual duties of maintaining the plane's ordnance, had taken on the role of chef. "You'll be pleasantly surprised when you open the box," he replied.

In earlier days, Johnson had been a little more daring in the culinary department, often preparing hot meals in a small galley stove at the rear of the plane. That changed when the plane experienced some negative Gs while a pot of peas was heating up on the stove. Suddenly there were peas all over the back of the plane. Since then, box lunches from the enlisted mess or K-rations had become the norm.

Sharman wanted to know if they had packed any more coffee. "We ran out up front during the last flight."

Johnson replied that he had a full two-pound can in back to share.

Wellman drank the coffee perked at ten thousand feet during patrols despite it being only lukewarm. He liked it hot, but coffee in any form helped keep him awake, and he would need it tonight because he hadn't gotten much sleep earlier that evening.

Night patrols were pretty much the rule lately; keeping alert could be a challenge. The boredom factor didn't help the situation. Most patrol flights were over ten hours long and not very exciting. Military experience has been described as "years of boredom interrupted by moments of excitement." That seemed an apt description of these patrols to Wellman.

The crew officers—pilot, co-pilot, and navigator—arrived and started going through the aircraft checkout procedures.

Lieutenant Kelly, the navigator on this flight, dropped a chronometer on the radio desk. Wellman got a time check and set the chronometer to Greenwich Mean Time. He then tuned the transmitter and checked his receivers.

The preflight chores were nearly finished when Lieutenant Peterson and four enlisted Electronic Reconnaissance spooks emerged from the darkness. They didn't participate in the preflight checkout. They picked up their survival kits and were ready to go. The ER people didn't have anything to do with flying the airplane. They were the payload. They all rode in the back section of the plane that was jammed full of electronic surveillance equipment. The enlisted ER people were mostly electronic technicians with special surveillance training. They bunked with the rest of the squadron's enlisted personnel but seemed a little distant. Like they knew something you didn't know, and they weren't going to tell you what that was.

One of the last things each crew member did was don an inflatable life jacket and strap on his front-carry parachute harness. The chutes were hung in various places about the plane and could be hooked onto the harness with two buckles.

The plane crew had finished their preflight chores and were on board and ready to go at 2130. It was dark and clear, no moon, although storms were expected along the China coast where they would be flying that night. The two reciprocating engines were started, the auxiliary power unit unhooked. A tow tractor pushed the plane back onto a taxiway where it could move under its own power. Lieutenant Colby sat in the right-hand seat of the cockpit as it taxied to the end of the runway and went through the pre-takeoff check list. Until recently, he had been the commander of this plane. He had piloted it since the navy accepted delivery from the factory two years earlier. It had been his plane, his crew. Tonight, he would be flying co-pilot.

Lieutenant Colby's ambition wasn't to be a hotshot navy pilot. He had no desire to be catapulted off a carrier or to land on a moving, pitching deck. His appearance reflected his modest demeanor. He was a little over-weight, not the sharpest-looking officer around, but an excellent pilot and plane crew commander.

Lieutenant Colby gravitated toward patrol aircraft out of flight school. He liked the planes' multiple engines, slow and steady. As an ensign, he spent time in a PBM seaplane squadron before moving on to the navy's latest land-based patrol plane, the P2V. He had qualified as a P2V com-mander and soon was promoted to lieutenant junior grade.

Not long after becoming a plane commander, Colby became aware that a US Navy "special project" was looking for volunteers. There weren't many details available, but it would be an overseas assignment requiring a two-year commitment, and applicants would have to qualify for high-level security clearance. The navy also favored volunteers who weren't married. Lieutenant Colby fit all the requirements and volunteered.

Lieutenant Colby and the other volunteers soon learned what the special project mission was. They would be part of an effort to assemble and deploy the navy's first dedicated airborne Electronic Reconnaissance capability. Two contingents were to be formed, with four planes each. One contingent would be stationed in North Africa and the other in the Philippines. Lieutenant Colby ended up in the Philippine four-plane contingent, which had the task of locating, monitoring, and categorizing electronic emissions along the Asian coastline from Saigon to Vladivostok.

It had turned out to be a good career move for the lieutenant. At a relatively young age, he was in command of an aircraft, the largest and most capable plane he had ever flown and was part of a mission that had a high priority in the post-World War II US Navy.

The crew had been pulled together two years earlier from various parts of the navy. They had become a cohesive unit that included a real hotshot co-pilot, who greased the plane in for landings so smooth they made Lieutenant Colby envious, and a smooth-faced ensign navigator who couldn't fly a plane for beans but got them to and from where they were going without getting lost.

The enlisted crew members were competent and reliable, and the group had remained pretty much intact while Lieutenant Colby was plane commander. However, changes were taking place, the inevitable result of the navy's rotation system, as well as personnel being released from service after fulfilling their obligations. Certain changes in the plane's officer complement had been devastating to Lieutenant Colby. His super-capable co-pilot left to return to civilian life as an airline pilot, and his baby-faced ensign navigator had also left the navy to pursue an advanced degree at Berkeley. At about the same time, the commanding officer of the special project was promoted from lieutenant to lieutenant commander and reassigned. He had been key in putting together the four planes, crews, and support personnel for the Philippine-based special project contingent. He had been a flying commanding officer and was probably the best pilot in the special project. His replacement, Lieutenant Commander Higgins, had a patrol plane background, but he had been flying a desk during his most recent assignments. Higgins needed some operational experience to advance his career, and the way the special project was set up also required him to be a plane commander. But for reasons that became obvious, Commander Higgins needed an experienced and able co-pilot. This was how Lieutenant Colby found himself in the right-hand seat of the cockpit he had been commanding for the past two years.

The pilots completed the pre-takeoff procedure, started the jets, lined up on the runway, and set the brakes. The two prop engines and jets were turned up to take-off power. When the brakes were released, the plane jumped forward and, even though fully loaded, lifted off quickly. It began climbing at a steep angle. The plane could out-climb and fly faster than most prop-driven fighters.

When the plane cleared Philippine air control boundaries, it went silent. No emissions would emanate except hourly encrypted Morse code position reports. Occasionally a nervous navigator might ask for a radar position check, but only as a last resort. The plane's mission was to receive and evaluate signals, not to emit them.

All crewmen actively involved in the plane's operation were tied into the plane's intercom system. Pilot radio voice communications could also be monitored on the intercom. At times the intercom was active with back-and-forth chatter, but in the middle of a night patrol it was most often quiet.

Shortly before the flight entered the on-station portion of the patrol, the navigator handed Wellman the first encrypted hourly position report to be sent to the navy patrol aircraft network in Morse code. Once the on-station point was reached, the external running lights were turned off and the gun turrets manned. The two radiomen and radar rotated in two-hour shifts to man the bow turret. The mechanic Scarma and the plane captain took turns in the top turret. Johnson, the ordnance man, handled the tail turret by himself.

The baby-faced, neat-as-a-pin navigator had been replaced by Lieutenant Junior Grade Kelly. Lieutenant Kelly had a slightly bulging midriff, and his clothes often looked as if they'd been slept in. The navigator's workspace, one of the roomier spaces in the plane, began to accumulate maps, scraps of paper, navigation instruments, coffee cups, and food droppings soon after Kelly settled in. However, so far, he'd always managed to find the way to where they were going and get them back again.

As the plane approached the China coast, the weather began deteriorating. Towering cumulus thunderheads outlined by flashing lightning filled the horizon. The air seemed to be filled with electricity; the plane became enveloped in Saint Elmo's fire, a spectacular phenomenon but not dangerous. Before Wellman ever witnessed Saint Elmo's fire, he had read about it occurring on sailing ships, when the rigging might be enveloped in the spectacle. However, Wellman had never seen a display of Saint Elmo's fire such as he was seeing now, and from the chatter on the intercom, it seemed that neither had anyone else. The electrically charged blue-tinted Saint Elmo's fire streamed off the wings. The plane's propellers looked like blue pinwheels. The navigator reported that the long-range LORAN navigation system had gone goofy, most likely due to the same phenomenon that was causing the Saint Elmo's fire.

A dark night, the darker the better, had become the favorite operational wish for the ER mission. This had not always been the case. When special project operations first started in 1951, flying the coastline from Shanghai south had been like a Sunday afternoon drive. Patrols flew around and inside the coastal islands on sunny afternoons. More care had to be taken around the Korean Peninsula and Vladivostok, but south of Shanghai had been a free-fly zone. That changed over time as more assets, in the form of MiG jets and radar detection systems, started appearing, particularly around Shanghai. Recently, all flights in the Shanghai area were scheduled for nighttime hours, as was this one.

North of Hong Kong, the patrol plane approached land and turned north to follow the coast in a driving rainstorm. The flight conditions were ideal for a plane that wanted to be inconspicuous, but a little tricky for the navigator. The plane's projected track ran twenty miles offshore. Making that turn using dead reckoning in a turbulent rainstorm required a lot of faith in dumb luck. A quick shot with the radar could have verified where they were located relative to the coast. But it could also announce their presence to the Chinese and pinpoint their location. Turning on the radar would indicate to the crew that the navigator didn't have a good handle on their location, which would have been accurate, but he would rather not admit it. Being a new kid on the block, Lieutenant Kelly didn't want to appear incompetent. For all those reasons, he did not ask for radar. He used dead reckoning plus a poor LORAN fix and hoped his guesses about wind speed and other variables were correct.

Kelly caught a break when they broke out of the storm and could see the surface about half an hour after making the turn. Bobbing lights indicated junks. There were other lights, too—not many, but enough to define the coastline's outer islands. The outer islands were close, too close; they were almost on top of them. Lieutenant Kelly made a correction to shift their track out to twenty miles, the intended distance offshore. That established the hourly position report that was transmitted back to naval operations in a coded message.

The break in the turbulent weather lasted a short time. Commander Higgins soon announced over the intercom that they were approaching another batch of storms. Sharman was in the process of handing Bailey, the radar man, coffee in a paper cup when the next turbulence hit, and he spilled half the cup on some papers on Bailey's desk. Bailey gave Sharman more than his normal surprised look, but since Sharman had his earphones on, which, combined with the plane's noise, made normal conversation difficult, he let it go at that. Bailey slurped down the remaining coffee and went forward to relieve MacBee, who was manning the bow turret.

The crew continued to be jostled for another hour as the plane plowed through storm after storm. They had flown halfway through the Formosa Strait before the storms abated. They found clear sky above and low clouds below. Lieutenant Kelly continued the struggle to pinpoint their location. He had managed to get a couple of low-quality LORAN fixes from transmitters located in Taiwan but questioned their reliability. He decided to do a celestial fix, not a common practice in the flying navy and not his strong suit in any case, but it could be a way to authenticate his LORAN fixes. Unfortunately, the celestial fixes didn't match the LORAN fixes. Lieutenant Kelly had to make a choice between two bad options and went with the LORAN fixes, based primarily on his lack of confidence in his celestial skills. Although different, both fixes shared one thing in common: they were running half an hour behind their expected schedule, which made the predawn schedule to clear the Shanghai area a little iffy.

Relieved that they had gotten through the turbulent weather, everyone fell into the rhythms of a routine patrol. Scarma, the flight mechanic, distributed box lunches and then relieved Sharman in the top turret. Sharman made yet another pot of coffee. Wellman swapped with Bailey in the bow turret, and MacBee took over the radio chores. The plane was controlled by auto pilot while the pilot and co-pilot worked on their box lunches and sipped on cups of the freshly made coffee. The navigator, still not happy with the plane's track, continued to fuss over his maps.

Low clouds persisted as the flight approached the Shanghai area. They would break away from the coast and head for Okinawa soon after passing Shanghai, but not before they cut through the edge of the waters designated as part of the Korean War zone. Flying over water in a war zone allowed each crew member to earn a chit that added to the twenty-five needed to earn an air medal for such activities. Medals were important to career officers.

It had been a quiet night for Lieutenant Peterson, who oversaw the electronic eavesdropping activities in the back of the plane. Normally the patrol wouldn't expect a lot of traffic in the ground they had covered, but things began picking up considerably as they approached Shanghai. The four technicians had been staring at mostly blank screens, kept alert in part by the rough weather they had been flying through. Now the screens were lighting up, as expected, and the barrage of electronic data had their full attention. In fact, the activity had picked up dramatically, and Lieutenant Peterson began to question what they were seeing. Something seemed strange. Lieutenant Peterson observed that a lot of the transmissions were coming from the east, which would be in the ocean. That wasn't impossible. They had learned early on that among the clutter of junks that filled the sea along the China coast, some that at first looked like one of the many were upon closer inspection bristling with antennas and emitting like mad. But what Lieutenant Peterson was seeing now seemed too persistent and too widespread to be attributed entirely to junk noise.

Lieutenant Peterson got on the intercom. "Navigator, this is ER. We seem to be getting some unusual activity, and it doesn't correlate with our position very well. Can you verify our position?"

Lieutenant Kelly saw this as an opportunity to get a radar fix and queried the pilot. "Commander Higgins, this is the navigator. Permission to turn on radar for quick verification of our position."

Higgins replied, "Can't you verify the position without radar?"

Lieutenant Kelly felt a need for further help from ER.

"ER, how important is your need for an accurate position right now?"

"This is ER. If you could see what we are seeing, you would want to know exactly where you are."

Some people would describe Commander Higgins as a nervous Nelly. The tone of Lieutenant Peterson's voice convinced him that turning on the radar would be a good idea.

Bailey fired up the radar. What Lieutenant Kelly observed took his breath away. The radar was set to read the surface below them for a range of fifty miles; Lieutenant Kelly could see nothing but land beneath the plane. They were at least fifty miles off track, somewhere northwest of Shanghai.

Lieutenant Kelly reported in an excited voice, "Pilot, we are off course and over land somewhere northwest of Shanghai!"

Commander Higgins had been tensing, but he wasn't ready for what he heard. He instinctively pulled back on the yoke, like he wanted to gain some altitude fast. The plane grabbed for altitude but with the low power settings flopped into a shallow stall. The engines surged as the propellers sought more resistance.

Plane captain Sharman and second radio MacBee, who had been listening to the conversation, looked at each other and rolled their eyes. Sharman leaned over and poked MacBee. "Bet we are waking up a bunch of villagers down there."

MacBee laughed. "Hope that's all we are waking up."

Commander Higgins came back on the intercom. "Navigator, give us a heading to get out of here, fast!" The navigator had apparently been thinking the same thing and immediately came back with a new heading. The plane banked sharply and headed toward the ocean and safety.

Another problem had become apparent. The flight was running behind schedule, and a hint of light toward the east announced the dawn of a new day.

Johnson, sitting in the tail turret listening to the intercom conversations, assessed the situation as he ate some chocolate he had saved from his box lunch. He checked to see that his twin twenty-millimeter cannons were ready if needed.

During the previous month one of the contingent's four planes had been jumped while flying a ligament track near Shanghai, off the coast. Two MiGs had made a firing pass. The pilot put the plane into a power-off diving turn. The MiGs made two more firing passes, but the turning plane made a difficult target, and the MiG pilots were likely inexperienced. The plane did not suffer any damage. The tail gunner used up most of his twenty-millimeter stores, also with no apparent effect. That attack had occurred in the morning, near daybreak.

Johnson considered the circumstances. The Chinese didn't have night fighter capabilities, but it had become light enough to launch daylight-capable fighter planes. Obviously, there were MiGs in the area; obviously radar had been tracking their lost flight. The chances of something bad happening were high. He began scanning the sky intently as visibility increased in the morning light. He told himself not to worry too much. If MiGs were around, they would make their presence known with guns blazing. Johnson's thoughts were interrupted by something moving high almost directly behind the him. He shouted into the intercom, "Tail to crew, I have something twelve o'clock high! They are closing. Two MiGs!"

Points of light erupted from the lead plane. Johnson pointed his sight at the flashes and fired a long burst from his twin twenty-millimeter cannons. The MiGs swept by. None of the other turrets got a fix on them.

Commander Higgins seemed frozen in place. He had been getting acquainted with the P4M flight procedures, including the unique circumstances associated with the mission. Higgins had flown several orientation flights, but this was his first experience as pilot and commanding officer during an operational patrol flight.

Before Lieutenant Colby requested permission to take control of the aircraft; he had already begun to act. He put the plane into a shallow dive and cranked up the jets. Under normal circumstances the procedure would be to drop down low over the water, but because the plane wasn't over water, Lieutenant Colby chose to dive into the cloud cover below them.

Radio always had an encoded attack message in a folder ready to send, and Lieutenant Colby ordered it sent. This would be followed by a position report supplied by the navigator. In this case, their position was slightly fudged to put them over water since they would be over water in a few minutes.

The cloud cover started breaking up about the time they reached the Yellow Sea. Lieutenant Colby took the plane down to three hundred feet above the surface to continue evasive action. The attackers hadn't returned after the first pass, probably discouraged when the P4M dove into the clouds.

After half an hour with the jets and military power on, the plane was taken back to its normal altitude and normal flight settings. It proceeded toward the Okinawa destination. They didn't have a choice—they couldn't continue burning fuel at the current rate and make it to Okinawa.

Apparently, the attack hadn't damaged the plane. Everything seemed to be working normally.

The plane's conventional prop engines had been operating faithfully all night, and the stress of being under full military power hadn't seemed to faze them. These engines were the most powerful and complex conventional engines the United States armed forces had ever put into service. Four banks of seven cylinders were ganged together to make a very powerful aircraft power plant that was also prone to reliability problems. A common problem with the engine involved the back-row cylinders fouling up. Once one of the cylinders stopped functioning it could become contagious and spread. These symptoms began to appear in the port engine. Power started to drop, and it became progressively worse. The crew members had experienced this kind of problem several times and so weren't particularly concerned. Lieutenant Colby consulted with Sharman, and they agreed the engine had to be shut down and the prop feathered. The crew made the necessary adjustments. The port jet was put into service to help the starboard engine carry the load.

The weather system they had been flying through all night now dominated Okinawa. As they approached the Okinawa air traffic control boundaries, the starboard engine blew. It wasn't the fouling problem experienced by the port engine. It was unexpected and unexplainable sudden failure. There hadn't been a decision to shut it down; it had shut down with no permission from anyone. The condition of the aircraft became perilous as it started losing altitude. Colby still had control of the plane, and Commander Higgins gave no hint that he would be resuming command. For all intents and purposes, Commander Higgins had become a passenger sitting in the pilot's seat. This was no longer an in-training patrol for Higgins.

The plane stabilized after the starboard jet came online. The crew's faces reflected the change from easygoing camaraderie to serious concern about the plane's survival. Wellman confirmed the location of his parachute, although bailing out over the ocean during a storm didn't seem like a good idea. Ditching a plane in a body of water was a perilous undertaking in any case; ditching in an agitated ocean offered a nearly zero chance of success. Better that Lieutenant Colby land this thing on terra firma.

Once the plane had lost both conventional engines, it had no generators. It now depended on batteries for electrical power. Fuel was another major concern. They were nearing the end of the flight. Most of their fuel would normally have been consumed by this time. However, they had used the jets over China, and they were burning even more fuel now by using the jets. The navigator calculated that the fuel remaining left no margin for circling or staying in the air above the airport. They had to go straight in.

The crew turned off everything electrical not needed to fly the plane or communicate. They used Morse code to inform Okinawa air traffic control of their predicament. They were cleared for a straight-in approach to a Kadena airport runway. Weather conditions were described as deteriorating, and they would be using a ground control approach (GCA) for the landing. That meant that a person on the ground would talk the plane in for the landing. As they approached the Kadena airport, very high frequency (VHF) communications were established with the control tower and GCA.

They lined up for the approach and moved into the glide path. Because of the driving rain and heavy wind squalls, visibility varied from insignificant to zero. The crew could hear the GCA voice directions on the intercom. The voice started off calm and reassuring, but as they descended, the corrections—were they right or left, above or below the glide path? —came faster and more urgently. The plane bobbed like a cork on an agitated pond. The GCA controller talked fast and sounded frantic when he shouted that they were 350 feet below the glide path and ordered them to pull up and go around. The crew listened to all of this on the intercom. There was a lot of puckering. They knew their fate depended on the skill of Lieutenant Colby. Lieutenant Colby ignored the GCA voice and somehow brought the plane back to the glide path before he smacked the plane down hard on the runway. Lieutenant Colby's usual landings weren't noted for their smoothness, so the landing could be classified as near normal.

When the plane rolled to a stop, the jet engines idled for a few minutes before the starboard engine stopped running, followed shortly by the port jet. They had burned the last fuel on board the aircraft and were blocking the main Kadena runway.

The storm continued to rage with heavy wind, rain, and flashing lighting. Emergency vehicles and fire trucks filled the runway, but there were no tow tractors among them. Lieutenant Colby informed the control tower that the plane had no power and couldn't taxi; it wouldn't be moving off the runway until a tow tractor showed up.

After the rough but safe landing on Mother Earth, the crew's anxiety dissipated. Abundant smiles and back slapping were occurring. They didn't mind one bit that they were temporarily stranded on Kadena's main runway in a rainstorm. Bailey, the radar man, asked Sharman what had happened to make the starboard engine quit the way it did. Sharman shrugged. "I hope everyone brought extra clothes, because if we have to change an engine, we'll be here for a while."

Finally, a tow tractor appeared. The driver and his helper, clothed in heavy rain gear, attached the tow bar and pulled the plane and crew to the parking spot where the local special project contingent waited in the pouring rain to greet them. Sharman dropped out of the plane, ducked under a wing to avoid the rain as much as possible, and supervised the chucking and tying-down process.

The contingent petty officer in charge approached him. He wore a poncho, and his face peeked out from under the hood. He asked the question that most concerned the men at the Okinawa outpost: "Hey, did you guys bring any mail?"

"You bet," Sharman replied. "We have your mail."

A year later Wellman, now a civilian making use of the GI Bill, checked his mail and found a letter from the US Navy.

It seemed that the navy had reviewed the events of the flight that got lost, was attacked by MiGs, and landed in a rainstorm with two engines out. The crew members had been awarded letters of commendation for meritorious achievement during aerial flight. In addition, Commander Higgins had been awarded a cluster to add to his air medal.

The way Wellman remembered it; their meritorious achievement involved surviving their own ineptitude. Somebody was sure gilding the lily, but he had to admit it had been one patrol that turned out to be less routine than most.

Photos on this page were taken by the author

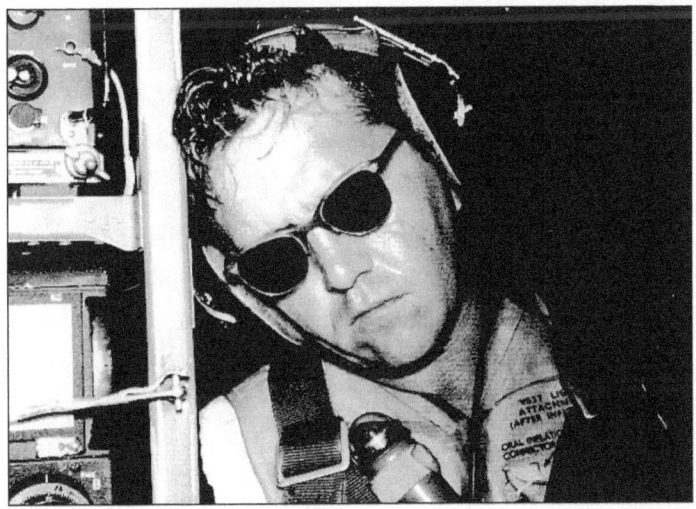

During long flights there would be time to socialize or catch a few winks

Addendum

The P4M-1Q, A Cold War Warrior

The P4M Mercator was a rare bird. There were two prototypes and nineteen production models. One of the production models, BuNo 121452, was lost in an accident in Chesapeake Bay on March 8, 1951. The other eighteen production models were converted to the P4M-1Q configuration to be used for the Electronic Reconnaissance mission.

From the 1950s through the 1970s when the Korean and Vietnam wars took place, the Cold War was at its peak. The peripheries of the communist nations were continually patrolled by United States Navy and Air Force aircraft. Sometimes these flights were intercepted, resulting in the deaths of two hundred navy and air force airmen in hostile actions. The public knew very little of this activity. As far as the United States government was concerned, it wasn't happening, so it couldn't protest if one of the reconnaissance aircraft that officially didn't exist was attacked or shot down.

The website *Intrusions, overflight, shoot downs and defections during the Cold War* (http://myplace.frontier.com/~anneled/ColdWar.html) attempts to list all the documented intercepts. The author of "US Naval Air: Routine Patrol" has found the website's list of intercepted intrusions and shoot downs voluminous but not complete. However, the site includes many pages and likely has listed most significant incidents. During 1952 and 1953, the period in which "US Naval Air: Routine Patrol" took place, there were thirty-two incidents of reported intercepts of aircraft flown by the United States and its allies near or within the borders of communist nations. Not many of these activities made the news; they were treated as top secret by the United States.

These numbers need to be put into perspective. During a two-year period starting in 1951 and ending in 1953, the author of "US Naval Air: Routine Patrol" flew on ninety-five patrols lasting approximately ten hours each. That is approximately fifty patrols a year. The four-plane contingent the author was associated with operated at about the same level and flew around two hundred patrols a year. That four-plane contingent was only a small portion of the overall reconnaissance activities occurring around the periphery of the communist nations at the time. In other words, the Electronic Reconnaissance experience was more boring than exciting. The most excitement occurred because of the weather or mechanical problems.

The author was aware of two intercepts involving the four-plane contingent while he was associated with it. One of the incidents has been listed in the *Intrusions, overflight, shootdowns and defections* website; the other one was not.

The one mentioned occurred April 23, 1953. US Navy plane BuNo 124369 was attacked by two MiG-15 Fagots while flying off the Chinese coast near Shanghai. The MiGs made several firing runs, and the crew of the P4M returned fire. The P4M was not hit, and as far as the crew could tell their return fire did not damage the MiGs.

A second incident is based on the excited talk of enlisted crew members who said they had been attacked by MiGs off Shanghai. The incident can't be found in any literature the author has seen, nor did the author see or hear anything confirming the attack at the time it occurred. The only source of information the author had at the time was the word of enlisted crew members.

These two incidents occurred within a month or two of each other. What were other P4M crew's reactions to this aggressive activity by the Chinese? The author can only speak for himself. One odd reaction, as he remembers it, was jealousy or envy of the crews that had experienced the attacks. "Why can't our crew have a little excitement once in a while?" Of course, the ideal scenario would have MiGs making multiple passes and never hitting a thing. The reality was that a lone patrol plane attacked by MiGs far from any assistance would have the odds stacked against it.

The author did have an opportunity to send an "under attack" message while on a patrol along the west coast of Korea. It was a dark night, and the ether was filled with a barrage of electronic activity. Things can get spooky under those kinds of conditions. The officer overseeing the Electronic Reconnaissance surveillance in the back of the plane suddenly excitedly reported that fire control radar had locked onto the plane. The pilot ordered the author to send the "under attack" message by Morse code and diverted the plane from its planned route. Nothing came of the incident except a debriefing when we returned to Atsugi Naval Air Station in Japan. The crew wasn't spouting off to anyone about how they had been attacked by a mysterious enemy on a dark night.

The author left the Sangley Point P4M contingent at the end of 1953, by which time it had been given the VQ1 squadron designation. In June 1955, VQ1 moved its operation to Iwakuni, Japan. While flying out of Iwakuni and Atsugi, VQ1 P4M-1Q aircraft were involved in two deadly intercept incidents. The first occurred August 22, 1956, when BuNo 124362 was attacked off Shanghai by Chinese MiG fighters. A Morse code message that they were under attack by enemy aircraft was received from the plane. That was the last message received from the plane. The crew of sixteen, four officers and twelve enlisted men, were lost. Search and rescue efforts recovered one body, and three more bodies were recovered later. The author saw a list of the crew members lost and knew one of the ER specialists who rode in the back of the plane. He had been part of the original P4M-1Q crews operating out of Sangley Point.

BuNo 124362 had also been involved in an attack a year earlier, as described by Jim Edison, the pilot. "I was the pilot of 124362 in the spring of 1955 when we were attacked about ten miles off Tsing Tau by two MiGs. It was a dark, clear night, and we were close enough to the airport to observe them take off and come straight at us. We did a power-off tight spiral to 300 feet while they fired 30 mm shells over the cockpit. Our tail gunner fired several hundred rounds in return. We kept turning under the MiGs and they appeared to lose track of us, and we departed at max speed, which was 385 knots. At the time, the Chinese were training in the MiGs, so that might explain their inability to press the attack. My aircraft, 124362, was later downed by the Chinese in 1956. I left the squadron a few months before that happened, and most of those lost were my crew. At that time, during those types of missions, we flew ten miles off the coast."

Another incident occurred on June 16, 1959, when two North Korean MiG-17 Frescos attacked P4M-1Q BuNo 122209, patrolling at seven thousand feet thirty miles off the east coast of North Korea. Pilot of the P4M-1Q was Commander Don Mayer, and Lieutenant Commander Vincent Anania was co-pilot. The tail gunner, PO2/c Corder, manned the pair of twenty-millimeter cannons. The MiG-17s closed rapidly and showed astonishingly good aim on their first pass. PO2/c Corder never had a chance to defend the plane; the first attack scored extensive hits across the Mercator's fuselage and wing. PO2/c Corder was hit badly, injured by over forty pieces of shrapnel that left him incapacitated. The P4M-1Q Mercator dropped down to just above the ocean. The MiGs came around, making more firing passes on the crippled plane. The engines on the starboard side were both disabled, and the rudder was badly damaged. The two port engines running at maximum power caused an asymmetric thrust, and the plane began to roll over. The mechanical controls were ill-suited to counteract the imbalance, and it took all the strength of the pilots keep the plane level. The MiGs made three firing passes before pulling up and turning back toward North Korea. The MiGs only had enough fuel capacity for short flights and likely broke off the attack in order to be able to return to their base.

The P4M-1Q had two engines out, a badly damaged rudder, and a fuselage and wing peppered with cannon rounds, but was still flying. It headed for the nearest friendly air facility in Japan, the Miho Air Force maintenance base. The plane made a successful landing at Miho. The wounded tail gunner survived. The P4M-1Q BuNo 122209 was determined to be unrepairable and was scrapped.

At the about the same time that the P4M-1Q contingent deployed to Sangley Point, another contingent of four P4M-1Q planes and their crews were deployed to NAS Port Lyautey, French Morocco. They patrolled European, Russian, and Iron Curtain borders to monitor electronic emissions.

As with the Far East contingent, there were likely many interesting unreported incidents during patrols of the Russian borders and countries under their control. However, none of the P4Ms were lost to adversarial actions. Two P4Ms were lost to other causes during the period they performed electronic monitoring in the European theater, one due to mechanical problems and the other to an accident.

On February 6, 1952, P4M-1Q BuNo 124371, staging out of Nicosia, Cyprus, was flying a track that took it to the Black Sea and along the coast of Ukraine. While over the Black Sea, the crew experienced a reciprocating engine failure and aborted the patrol. A jet was utilized to compensate for the lost engine as the plane headed back to Cyprus. Mountains over eight thousand feet high lay ahead. The jet couldn't provide enough power to top the mountains, and the plane had to fly between the mountains on its return trip. The jet had also consumed more fuel than would normally be used. As they approached Cyprus, they ran out of fuel and made a dead-stick landing in high-sea conditions east of Cyprus. Fourteen of the fifteen men on board managed to launch a raft and get free of the plane. After the raft was launched, the aircraft commander returned to the plane for some reason and was lost. The other crew members were rescued by the British *HMS Chevron* after floating for several hours in the heavy sea that made it difficult to locate them.

On January 6, 1958, a VQ-2 P4M-1Q was being flown from Port Lyautey, Morocco, to Norfolk, Virginia, for the complete checkup required after accumulating a certain number of hours. Nearing its destination, the P4M crashed at Ocean View, Virginia. Four crewmen were killed and two survived. Three civilians were injured. The cause of the accident was never determined.

The P4M-1Q planes were withdrawn from service in 1960. Though their service life was short, they had contributed much to the nation in the early days of the Cold War. A total of eighteen P4Ms had been converted to the 1Q version for use in electronic surveillance warfare. Four of the P4M-1Q planes were lost, two after being attacked, one to mechanical problems, and the fourth to an accident.

Memphis 1948

Picture is in the public domain

Author's Foreword

I attended aviation electronics classes at the Naval Air Technical Training Center near Memphis in 1948. At the time, the United States military services were becoming fully integrated, while the South, including Memphis, remained fully segregated as defined by Jim Crow laws. This resulted in conflicting practices in how people of different races interacted depending if they were located inside the Naval Technical Training Center or outside it.

I had grown up in rural South Dakota and never had contact with non-white people of any kind before entering the navy. I remember seeing only one black person in the town near our farm before I left in my late teens. The separation of races—separate drinking fountains, separate restrooms, separate eating facilities—bothered me, but I had no experience with living in a society where racial differences existed. I didn't feel qualified to comment on the practice of Jim Crow laws, but I did feel uncomfortable with the practice of segregation. On its face, it seemed immoral and conflicted with many of the basic principles on which our country had been founded, like all men are created equal. My memories of that 1948 experience are the basis for this story.

Memphis 1948

Isaiah and his wife Sarah, sharecroppers who lived in the Mississippi Delta, farmed twenty-four acres of cotton on land owned by Ed Sharpton. They had one son, Tyler

Isaiah was a descendent of three generations of the Williams family who had lived in the Mississippi Delta as slaves, field hands, landowners, and, finally, sharecroppers. Isaiah's father, whose parents had been enslaved, worked as a field hand and accumulated enough money and good enough credit to buy eighty acres of rich Delta land. Isaiah inherited the eighty acres with an outstanding mortgage in 1915, a time when Negroes were facing increasing political pressure and finding it difficult to obtain credit. At one time in the late 1800s, Negroes owned two-thirds of the Delta. By the 1920s they had lost most of it. In 1920, Isaiah lost his farm and became a sharecropper.

During this time, Ed Sharpton was buying up land lost by bankrupt Negroes, using credit unavailable to them. Ed claimed his great-grandfather had been a general in the Confederate Army, a common claim in the South at the time. With all those generals, one would think the South would have won the war. If Ed's great-grandfather had been a general, Ed hadn't inherited characteristics one associated with a general. He was short of stature and skinny, with poor posture. His face had a hawk-like appearance: narrow lips, beaked nose, small eyes.

Ed Sharpton had been working deals since he was in grade school. Most of his deals had gone nowhere but buying up distressed farmland seemed to be paying off. In order to utilize the land, he had accumulated, he broke it into small plots for sharecroppers to farm. Ed furnished the land, a mule, plows, other tools to work the land, seed and fertilizer, and a shack without electricity or running water for the sharecropper's family to live in. For this he received half of whatever the sharecropper produced on the land. Ed wouldn't let the sharecroppers use any of the land for a garden. All the land had to go into cotton. In addition, all the sharecroppers' shacks were bunched together, with no room for yards or gardens. The shacks were part of a hamlet that included mule barns, sheds filled with plows and other field tools, and a warehouse for fertilizers and seeds. Also, in the hamlet was a store owned by Ed Sharpton where sharecroppers bought necessities.

Each year the crop yield depended on many variables, such as the amount of rainfall, if boll weevils were a problem, if plant diseases affected the crop, or if Ed provided enough fertilizer. When the crop was harvested at the end of the year, Ed Sharpton would buy the Williams family's share of the crop at a price determined by Ed. What the family received at that time was their only source of income until the next harvest.

If the money ran out before the next harvest, the family had only one place to get credit to buy necessities—the store Ed Sharpton ran. As a result, most or all the Williams family's share of a year's crop might be needed to pay for the necessities they had bought on credit during the previous year.

In the spring of 1940, Isaiah was in his fifties. He was all bone and muscle, but slightly stooped over. He had turned prematurely gray and lost most of his teeth, and his face was wrinkled from spending many years working the fields in the heat of summer. Sarah was only a few years younger than Isaiah but didn't display the signs of aging in the way Isaiah did. Her face was smooth and her hair a mass of black ringlets. Not that Sarah didn't work hard. During the summer and fall, she hoed and picked cotton beside Isaiah, as well as cooking for the family and washing their clothes by hand in a wash tub. Sarah was just one of those people who didn't seem to age. Tyler appeared to be a typical eleven-year-old boy, a string bean who couldn't get enough to eat. However, to someone who knew him well, he wasn't a typical eleven-year-old boy. He had the bright shining eyes of youth but often looked beyond where there was anything to see, and his mind also seemed focused on that far-off place.

As an eleven-year-old, Tyler worked in the fields. Tyler's father, Isaiah, had gone to school for four years and had a rudimentary ability to read and do figures. Sarah had never attended school. Despite this meager experience with education, the pair made certain that Tyler went to the one-room, one-teacher school for Negroes where grades one through six were taught. Other sharecroppers often sent their children to the school when they didn't have anything better for them to do. Tyler's parents sent him because they wanted him to learn. It worked out well, because Tyler liked school and wanted to learn.

Sarah wanted her boy to go to school, as most mothers did. Isaiah had a more personal reason for wanting Tyler to go to school. Isaiah believed he had lost his farm in part because he had an inadequate education. He signed contracts he couldn't read and knew nothing about the laws that allowed his farm to be taken away from him. He didn't want that to happen to his son.

The school was a shack similar to those the sharecroppers lived in. Miss Brown, a black woman, was the teacher. She was big and had an attitude. Her wardrobe was limited, but she managed to dress neatly in a clean dress every day. Miss Brown had been teaching single-room, multiple-class schools for fifteen years before taking over the sharecropper school. She maintained order and discipline by doing whatever the situation required, and students who didn't understand this soon became educated. For this she had the use of one of the sharecropper shacks and was paid ten dollars in cash each month and given twenty dollars' worth of credit to buy supplies and food from Ed's store.

Despite her rough exterior, Miss Brown loved every child she ever taught, and Tyler was no exception. However, Tyler was exceptional, the best student she had ever had. That became apparent soon after he started first grade. He wanted to know everything about everything and had the capacity to absorb all the knowledge Miss Brown could provide. Miss Brown's concern was that what she could provide was limited by her abilities and the school's resources. The school used twenty-year-old workbooks designed for children learning to read and do basic arithmetic. They were not books filled with the knowledge that Tyler needed. Miss Brown had been around long enough to know that talking to the county superintendent would be like talking to the sky: a waste of time. As an alternative, Miss Brown decided to talk to Ed Sharpton.

Ed Sharpton spent a lot of his time in the store, and Miss Brown approached him there one day about the school's needs.

"Mr. Ed," Miss Brown said, "I know you're interested in educatin' sharecropper children. Always said you were. I'd like to thank you for that. Now, I have this problem that you kin help on. I need more books. Some of da high grades need books 'bout history, geography, grammar, things like that."

Ed laughed. "Niggers don't need anythin' but learnin' how to read a little an' some 'rithmetic. You don't wanna put fancy ideas in their heads." With those words Ed left the store to tend to something.

Miss Sally Bates, the white woman who tended the store six days a week, spoke up after Ed left. Miss Bates and Miss Brown had become casual friends. Miss Brown came into the store often to pick up groceries and other items, and if things were slow at the store, as they often were, they enjoyed visiting for a while.

"Miss Brown," Miss Bates said, "Maybe I can help you. I use the library in Clarksdale, and I can borrow up to three books at a time for three weeks. I don't have that much time to read, so I could help you with two books every three weeks."

"Miss Bates," Miss Brown replied, "that'd be so kind and so helpful."

The two women huddled and decided what kind of books to borrow. This unlikely partnership continued for the last three years that Tyler attended the sharecropper school. Older students who were interested had their education enhanced by the borrowed books too.

In the spring of 1940, Tyler was eleven and finishing the sixth grade when Isaiah decided they should leave the Delta. Isaiah's brother Howard had moved to Chicago the year before and gotten work in a factory making auto parts. Howard wrote, "There is plenty work for them wants to work and the pay is good."

The Williams family had been living in the Delta for generations; Isaiah and Sarah knew nothing else. When they'd owned the farm, it had been a satisfying life. Sharecropping was a setback with no future, and the oppression of the Negro race in Mississippi continued to increase. The information from Howard, if half true, meant an improvement over their present situation. Isaiah didn't have a hard time convincing Sarah that they should break their bonds with the Delta and leave the unsatisfying known in hopes of finding a better life in the unknown.

Late one night that spring, they packed everything they would take with them into a relative's car. It took them to Clarksdale, where they caught the train to Chicago, leaving behind the life they knew and their unpaid debt at Ed Sharpton's store.

They moved in with Howard's family while Isaiah looked for work and the family became acquainted with Chicago. In the evening over dinner, Howard would fill them in on things he had learned about the neighborhood. "They's good, they's bad, but better than the Delta for sure. They's still segregation—not Jim Crow, but still segregation," he said. "Ya can't live just anyplace, only places where Negroes live. Da schools where Negroes live, dey not much better than da Negro Delta schools. Po' teachers, po' everythin.'"

Isaiah was disappointed to hear most Chicago schools in Negro neighborhoods were no better than in the Delta. They were not officially segregated, but in practice they were. Isaiah didn't know all the reasons why, but Howard said they were, and he believed his brother.

Isaiah decided to find out what he could expect from Chicago schools. Isaiah knew Tyler was a smart boy. Miss Brown had told him Tyler was the smartest student she'd ever had, and Isaiah wanted to get Tyler in a school where he could make use of those smarts and learn as much as he could. Isaiah started talking to people who knew things about education.

He talked to the preacher at Howard's church. The preacher didn't have a high opinion of schools in the community where his flock lived. "They's bad schools and they's worse ones. Da children spend the day there but don't see them learnin' anything."

He visited a neighborhood school. It was summer, so the principal had time to talk. The principal, a white man, didn't talk up his school, didn't talk up the Chicago school district. He talked about problems. It didn't seem like the principal was talking to Isaiah. Isaiah happened to be an object the principal could use to unload his frustrations. He talked about the huge influx of Negroes from where Isaiah was from and other places in the South. They had to live somewhere. When the Negroes moved into a neighborhood, the white folks moved out, often to the suburbs. The Negroes didn't have the wealth the whites moving out had. The Negroes moving in had many educational needs while the district's finances were deteriorating.

Isaiah wasn't understanding everything the principle was saying but he understood that the Chicago school district had big problems and wouldn't be a good place for a Negro, especially Tyler, to go to school.

A friend visiting Howard planted an idea in Isaiah's mind. The friend lived in Joliet, a community on the southwest edge of Chicago. The friend told Isaiah that there was a Negro community in the middle of Joliet, compact and segregated just like the neighborhoods in Chicago, which were the only places Negroes could rent or buy a house. The elementary school in the Negro community had mostly Negro students and struggled with staffing and lack of support. However, there were only two middle schools and one high school in the district, and they were integrated because there was no other option.

Joliet wasn't far from where Howard lived, so Isaiah took a bus to visit the city and check out job opportunities. Good-paying jobs weren't plentiful, but there was work. The result was that the Williamses moved into the Negro community in Joliet, where Isaiah found work as a janitor. Tyler entered middle school the next fall.

Tyler spent the next six years in Joliet schools and graduated from high school with almost perfect grades despite some teacher's reluctance to give him the grades he deserved. However, the school would not allow Tyler to be named valedictorian. That would stretch tolerance beyond reasonable limits.

Tyler's graduation from high school had been the goal for Tyler's parents. The goal had been met. Now what? Neither Isaiah, Sarah, nor Tyler had given that much thought. Despite being at the top of his class, opportunities for a Negro were limited. Few jobs were open to Negroes that provided more than the lowest level of pay for unskilled work. Negroes were the cleanup people in service businesses; in manufacturing they worked assembly lines and did work other people didn't want to do. In the construction business Negroes provided unskilled labor.

College for Tyler was really beyond Isaiah and Sarah's level of comprehension. Tyler had a broader understanding of the education hierarchy, but he also understood that neither he nor his family had the means to consider college an option. He thought about what his real options were. The most likely would be a manufacturing job. It didn't take long for him to find work in Joliet on an assembly line. He continued to live at home and contributed to family expenses.

Tyler did not aspire to working on an assembly line for the rest of his life. Tyler had been worrying about his options for almost two years when a fellow assembly line worker named Clayton informed him that he would be leaving soon to go into the navy. Tyler was surprised by Clayton's announcement. "Going into the navy?" Tyler questioned. "The navy don't take Negroes."

"Well, they's taking me," Clayton replied. "Not a steward polishin' officers' shoes, but a real sailor. Something 'bout an executive order Truman usin' says the navy has ta take any citizen meets the requirements. Skin color's not one of 'em. Be going up ta Great Lakes boot camp nex' week."

Tyler didn't question Clayton's veracity, but, curious by nature, he decided to check out for himself what was going on with discrimination in the navy. After a few hours at the library, Tyler had found the source of the change. In 1947, President Truman had interpreted Executive Order 8802, signed by President Roosevelt in 1941, as the basis to begin ending discrimination in the armed forces. Then that year, in 1948, Truman issued his own executive order 9981 to make it clear that there would be no more discrimination in the armed forces of the United States. Apparently, this executive order was working for Clayton.

That the navy was accepting Negroes as recruits opened up a possibility that Tyler hadn't considered. He hadn't seen much of the world other than the Mississippi Delta and Joliet, Illinois. His future so far seemed limited to low-level jobs, no matter what field he worked in.

He talked to his parents. Isaiah and Sarah had long ago decided that they could give Tyler support and love, but he was more capable than they were in just about any subject they could think of. "You decide for yourself," Isaiah said. "You know more about it than most folks do."

Tyler had never considered joining the armed services an option. He had heard that, with few exceptions, Negroes in World War II were used in all-Negro units and mostly in noncombatant roles. The thought of a segregated, separate but equal type of military organization turned him off. The idea of Negroes serving in the military confined to their own toilet facilities, own mess halls, separate barracks, and maybe colored-only fox holes seemed ridiculous to him. If, as Clayton said, Negroes were being accepted to serve in an integrated navy, that could be a be a different story.

Tyler stopped in the navy recruitment office in Joliet. A lone man in a uniform sat at a desk drinking coffee and reading a newspaper. A half-eaten donut sat on a napkin beside the coffee cup. The man didn't project the image in recruiting posters. He slouched over the desk, was a little flabby, and his uniform could have used a good pressing. The man glanced up and then resumed reading the newspaper. Tyler stood waiting to be recognized.

After a few minutes he realized that he was being ignored.

"Sir," Tyler said, "I would like to ask a few questions."

"About what?" the man asked.

"Well, I heard that Negroes could enlist in the regular navy now."

"What do you mean, regular navy?" the man in the recruiting office asked. "Negroes have always been able to enlist as stewards. You want to be a steward?"

Tyler was becoming irritated. He knew he was getting the runaround. This man didn't want him in his office and didn't want Tyler to be in the navy. Tyler reacted in kind. He wasn't going to be intimidated. "No," Tyler said. "I don't want to be a steward. I want to be in the regular navy as a deck hand or whatever regular sailors do."

"What makes you think you can enlist in the regular navy?"

Tyler, struggling to remain calm, answered, "A friend of mine has enlisted in the regular navy and will be going to the Great Lakes boot camp next week."

The man in uniform had a scowl on his on his face, but his mind was working on a different problem. He was a recruiting officer whose job was to encourage men to join the US Navy. The goal for the number of men he was to recruit that month was far from filled. As a recruiting officer, he had been informed he could recruit Negroes. He didn't like to see Negroes serving in the navy, but there wasn't much he could do about that. What he could do was sign this Negro up. It would increase his number of recruits for the month, no matter what color the man was. He reached into a drawer, pulled out some papers, and asked Tyler if he could read or write.

Tyler didn't respond to the question.

"In any case," the recruiting officer said, "you can take these papers home, get some help if need be, and bring them back with a certified birth certificate."

Tyler asked the recruiting officer if he had something to write with. "I'll fill out the papers now." Tyler hadn't intended to enlist that day, if ever, but he was so ticked off he decided to do it right there in front of the recruiting officer so he could see Tyler reading and writing.

Tyler filled out the forms quickly and handed them to the surprised recruiting officer, who noted how quickly and neatly the forms had been filled out. "Well, very good," the recruiting officer said. He reminded Tyler to bring in a birth certificate and handed him a card with the date and place he was to go for the physical.

From that point the process moved along quickly. Tyler passed the physical and was told to report to the Chicago City Center recruiting office in two weeks when a group of navy recruits would assemble to be transported to the Great Lakes Navy Training Center boot camp. Two weeks later twelve nervous, anxious young men were herded into a conference room. A navy officer had the men stand up and face him. He said something about swearing in and had the men raise their right hands and repeat after him the enlisted men's oath. They all did that, and the officer said the men were now United States naval recruits. "Good luck."

When the recruits arrived at boot camp, they were outfitted with uniforms and assigned to a fifty-man company. In the integrated company, Tyler and five other Negroes were part of the otherwise all-white unit.

The first week's training proceeded with a heavy emphasis on the importance of discipline, which included close-order drills as an example. The navy chief petty officers responsible for training the recruits used whatever means necessary to shape them up to march in step and react to verbal commands without stumbling over each other. The half-dozen Negroes were not singled out from the rest of the company. From Tyler's perspective, it appeared that discipline was applied where needed; color wasn't a factor.

After a long day of drilling, training, and classes, the recruits would return to the barracks to clean up, wash their clothes, get themselves ready for the next day's activities, and maybe find a little time to relax.

There were several southern white boys in the company who Tyler would label as rednecks in their natural environment. Some of them didn't hide their disdain for the Negroes in the company. This became apparent soon after the company had formed and moved into the barracks.

Two long tables with benches where recruits could write letters, shine their shoes, or just hang out in the middle of the company barracks. A Negro recruit sat down at one of the tables to write a letter. Two southern white boys were shining their shoes at the other table. One of the southern boys remarked that he didn't know niggers could write. The Negro recruit reacted instantly, picked up the uncapped ink bottle he was using and flung it at the two southern recruits. The ink bottle hit one of them and spilled ink over both rednecks and across the table. The southern recruits jumped up and lunged after the ink thrower, tipping over the table he was sitting at.

"You son of a bitch!" one of the rednecks yelled. "We are going to skin your black ass."

The ink thrower stood up and was ready to do battle. Tyler and the rest of the company were drawn to the chaos of tipping furniture and yelling. Tyler, instinctively sensing this could not be allowed to continue, grabbed the Negro recruit. Other recruits, following Tyler's example, grabbed the two rednecks. What could have escalated into a larger race-incited incident cooled down. They tried to clean up the mess, but there was no way all traces of what had happened could be erased.

The following morning, the chief petty officer in charge of the company learned the whole story. The morning's training schedule was altered. The company stood at attention in front of the barracks while a navy officer lectured them on Presidential Executive Order 9981, which ended segregation in the United States Armed Services. The officer ended with this warning: "It is the law. If you break the law, you will be prosecuted, and if found guilty, punished, and will at a minimum be given a dishonorable discharge. When the commander in chief, the president, issues an order, you better damn well obey it if you want to serve in the United States Navy. We are going to overlook what happened last night, but if it or anything like it happens again in this company, there will be consequences."

There were other no racially motivated disturbances during the remainder of boot camp.

Boot camp tested the recruits physically and mentally. They were required to meet certain strength, flexibility, and third-class swimmer standards. Anyone falling short of meeting the physical requirements received individual training in order to meet the requirements before leaving boot camp. Tests to determine math, reading, and general knowledge levels were administered. At the end of boot camp, each recruit was interviewed and informed about what options were available to that recruit based on his background, test scores, and related capabilities.

The interviewer, Josh Brisson, watched as Tyler approached his desk. Josh didn't spend a lot of time with each recruit and sometimes hadn't looked at the recruit's file until the interview. Josh was surprised to see Tyler was a Negro. He hadn't interviewed any Negroes before, although he knew Negroes were now allowed to serve in any capacity in the navy. Josh had grown up in rural Wisconsin and had never known or had contact with Negroes. He went into the navy from the farm; it had been an all-white organization until then. The Negro walking toward him made a good physical impression: trim, good posture, pleasant looking. The deep tan skin enhanced his impression of a handsome young man.

Tyler stood in front of the desk, and Josh gestured for him to sit down. "Excuse me," Josh said to Tyler. "Give me a minute to look through the file." What Josh saw in the file was evidence of an obviously sharp recruit. This contradicted what Josh had heard about Negroes; he struggled to get his head around what he now saw. To place recruits in slots where they would best fill the navy's needs, interviewers had guidelines to follow. It was the interviewer's responsibility to select candidates, based on their capabilities, to be trained fill those needs. The navy was a technology-oriented fighting force and needed large numbers of skilled personnel to operate and maintain complex facilities, ships, submarines, and aircraft. The evidence in front of Josh indicated this recruit should be guided into one of the demanding skills most needed by the navy.

Josh looked up from the file. "Very impressive. You are qualified to go into any rating you're interested in. What are you thinking about? What would you like to do in the navy?"

Tyler studied the interviewer. "I get to pick what I want to do?"

"In your case, that is true," Josh replied. "Are you interested in shipboard duty, aircraft, or submarines? Those are the categories to choose from, and then you decide what you want to do in the category."

World War II had only recently ended, and Tyler had become fascinated with aircraft and their use during war. The Tuskegee pilots were his heroes. "I'd like to have something to do with aircraft," Tyler replied.

"There is a full set of navy ratings related to aircraft maintenance and operation," Josh explained. "The rating I would like you to consider is aviation electronics technician. You will get almost a year of training, and if you do well, you can come out as a third- or second-class petty officer. Some enlisted sailors spend years and never make second-class petty officer."

Tyler took the recommendation and found himself at the Memphis Tennessee Naval Aviation Training Station attending aviation electronics technician school. He was in a class of twenty, the only Negro in the class. Not surprising, since few Negroes had been accepted into the navy at that point in time.

Tyler encountered bigotry at the Memphis Naval Air Station, the kind that any Negro would consider normal. Otherwise, the Memphis Naval Air Station was fully integrated. Off the base, however, the state of Tennessee and city of Memphis were a different matter. To Tyler, Jim Crow seemed more prevalent in Memphis than it had been in the Delta.

Tyler found the training interesting and not difficult. He graduated, as had become normal for him, at the head of the class. He had the petty officer second-class rating sewed onto his uniforms and decided to celebrate by going into Memphis to spend some time on Beale Street. He'd go alone. Of the few Negroes on the base, Tyler found none who shared common interests. None of his white classmates would want to go with him, and Tyler didn't fault them for that. Sailors of different races together on a Memphis street could draw a crowd.

Tyler wore his dress blue uniform with the new second-class rating on the sleeve. He caught a navy bus that circulated through the base and then made a run to Memphis. The bus was nearly empty, and Tyler took a seat behind the bus driver. When the bus got to the main gate a marine guard stepped on board and checked the servicemen's liberty passes. When the marine had finished checking the passes, the driver stood up and said, "All you colored folks now have to move to the back of the bus." Tyler, the only Negro on the bus, stood and moved to the back of the bus.

After completing his training, Tyler was assigned to a unit at Miramar Navy Air Station near San Diego, testing high-definition radar being developed to detect snorkeling submarines. Navy technicians were working with civilian engineers to get the kinks out of the new radar before it was deployed for fleet use.

Tyler found the work interesting and challenging. The radar guys were more interested in the technology than in skin color, and there wasn't any obvious bigotry in the group. One of the sharpest technicians he worked with was a first-generation Mexican American. Tyler got to do some flying when testing the equipment, something he liked, and it also made him eligible for flight pay.

Tyler had finished his second year of a three-year enlistment when the Korean War broke out.

The navy was interested in using their new radar for airborne command and control operations, and Korea offered a chance to test its applicability under realistic conditions. As a result, a contingent from the Miramar radar group, including Tyler, was sent to Japan to test the radar's command and control capabilities while flying over Korea and adjacent waters. During this deployment, Tyler became aware that the GI Bill that had assisted World War II veterans wanting to attend college was being extended to Korean veterans. Now Tyler knew what he would be doing after completing his navy enlistment, an enlistment extended for a year because of the Korean War. He would attend the University of Illinois at Urbana, a school that admitted Negroes, to major in electrical engineering,

Once at the University of Illinois, Tyler changed his major to physics, a change endorsed by his advisor. This was driven by Tyler's interest in the physical world beyond electricity and its various forms. He graduated with honors from the University of Illinois and went on to earn a master's degree and doctorate in physics from the Massachusetts Institute of Technology. He then became a research scientist at Stanford University.

Tyler's world had changed dramatically since he left Joliet. He was now a respected PhD conducting research at Stanford. The Civil Rights Act had been enacted in 1964. which Tyler considered long past due, although he had no illusions that that the act would immediately eliminate prejudice or bigotry in America.

All these changes did not cause Tyler to forget or ignore his parents, who still lived in Joliet. He not only respected and loved them but was grateful for what they had done to be sure he became educated to the best degree they could provide. They had started him on the path that carried him to where he was today.

Tyler visited Isaiah and Sarah often. They were now in their early eighties, both still in good health. They were proud to be independent and self-sufficient. Tyler had helped them buy a home they loved in a still-segregated part of Joliet.

Once while visiting Isaiah and Sarah, Tyler suggested taking a car trip together. They'd follow the Mississippi River down to Memphis. "We can take our time, visit sites along the way."

Isaiah wanted to know why they'd want to go to Memphis. "Remember?" Tyler answered, "I spent time there when I was in the navy, and I wonder if things have changed much."

Isaiah and Sarah agreed it could be interesting. They spent a day preparing and then began the road trip following the Mississippi River. Their first stop was in Galina, Illinois, a well-preserved historic town near the Mississippi River. They visited several other historical sites, including Hannibal, Missouri, the home of Tom Sawyer, as they leisurely moved south. When they reached Memphis, Tyler suggested they ride a bus. Isaiah didn't understand why Tyler wanted to ride a city bus. "I ride them all the time in Joliet."

Isaiah and Sarah relented, and they caught a city bus. They didn't know where it was going, but Tyler said it didn't matter. The bus wasn't crowded. They sat right behind the driver. Tyler smiled to himself, remembering having to move to the back of the bus when it'd left the Naval Air Station in 1948 on the way to Memphis.

Tyler looked for Whites or Negroes Only signs while riding the bus. He didn't see any.

The bus happened to stop in front of the Peabody Hotel. "Let's eat in the Peabody," Tyler said. "It's about time for lunch."

Tyler and his parents walked into the hotel toward the large dining room adjacent to the lobby. The Peabody, an historic hotel in downtown Memphis, had experienced its up and downs. In 1948 it had been out of bounds for black folks. Now there didn't appear to be any black folks dining, but the people waiting on tables were black, as was the pretty young black lady who greeted them when they walked in.

"Table for three?" the pretty lady asked.

"Yes," Tyler replied, "over by the window."

"There will be a little wait," the pretty lady replied. "We need to clear a table."

As they drove back to Joliet, Tyler reminisced. Yes, Memphis had changed drastically over a short period of time. More than Joliet, where discrimination was always under the surface. But he was encouraged that change was possible; he could feel it, see it, in Memphis.

Unintended Heroes

Milbank Main Street

Unintended Heroes

Peter Houser used a scoop shovel to finish cleaning the barn gutter. Peter, called Pete by people who knew him, had been doing most of the cow chores on the Houser farm since he finished eighth grade in the one-room school half a mile down the road. Now nineteen, he had become a strapping, well-muscled six-foot-tall young man. He pushed the wheelbarrow filled with the steaming sloppy mess out the barn door into the cold February air and dumped the load on the winter's accumulation of frozen manure.

Pausing for a moment, he watched as thirty Holstein cows wandered around the yard or lined up to drink from an insulated water tank prevented from freezing by an electric heater. He had let the cows out of the barn for their daily dose of fresh air and the freedom to move about for a while. The temperature lingered in the single digits; he would let them back into the warm barn after an hour or two.

Pete spread fresh straw on the concrete pad where the cows were kept in place by steel stanchions for most of the day during the winter. When he finished, he observed the clean barn with satisfaction.

Pete's dad came into the barn through a side door. Emil Houser stood short and sturdy, his square German face perpetually tanned from long days outdoors. He wore his winter chore uniform—a flannel-lined denim jacket and ear-lapper cap, long johns under his overalls, and a blue denim shirt, the same kind of overalls and shirt he wore every day of the year except when going to church.

Emil informed Pete he would be going to the sale today with a pickup load of sows. From late fall to early spring, the Milbank sale barn had a sale every Saturday afternoon. Emil often went to the sale barn on Saturdays to sell or just socialize. "You can help me load the pickup," he said. "Then maybe open up one of those alfalfa stacks. The haymow is getting pretty empty."

Pete had just had his work plan laid out for the day. Since finishing the eighth grade, Pete had been what amounted to a full-time hired man on the Houser farm, located in northeastern South Dakota, halfway between Milbank and Wilmot. Except he didn't think of himself as a hired man. For one thing, he didn't get paid regularly, and he felt he had a vested interest in the farm. It had always been his expectation that he would run it someday. His sixteen-year-old brother might be assuming the same thing, but Harold was going to high school and had other possibilities.

During the past year or so, Pete had been questioning his future expectations, wondering if they were realistic. His dad had just turned fifty and would be running the show for a long time, maybe longer than Pete would want to work as an unpaid hired man. His dad had lived through some hard times. Pete didn't know all the details, but he knew that the farm they lived on had been homesteaded by his grandfather in the late 1800s. His dad took over the farm in the 1920s and mortgaged the homestead to purchase an additional 160 acres. Shortly after he got the loan to buy the extra land, the economy went south. Insult had been added to misery when the worst drought anyone had ever seen kicked in; the only thing that grew were Russian thistles. Dust storms became common.

The original homestead and the additional 160 acres were lost. The local bank that had foreclosed on the farm went bankrupt soon after that, and the title ended up in the hands of a Connecticut insurance company. An old German farmer who lived up the road from the Housers said it wouldn't have been so bad if they hadn't had the Depression and hard times both at the same time.

Things started to get better in the late thirties, got really good during

World War II, and kept going good after the war. In the early forties, Pete's dad bought the farm back from the insurance company, which had never wanted to own it in the first place. Since then, Emil had replaced the horses with tractors and added a silo to the barn. A machine shed had been built for all the new machinery. The house had been remodeled and wired for electricity and plumbed for running water. Things were much better for the Houser family, but Emil still rigorously guarded every penny and every possession.

Knowing all this didn't make it any easier for Pete to ask to use the Studebaker, the first new car the Houser family had ever owned, the car his dad had treated like a crown jewel since he brought it home the previous fall. As much as Pete hated going through the ritual of asking for the car, he had to since it was his turn to drive when he and his friend, Chris Engelson, and his cousin, Lyle Houser, went for their weekly Saturday night outing. Chris and Pete had been in the same grades in their one-room country school for eight years and knew each other really well.

"My turn to drive again," he said hesitantly to his father.

"Seems like you just drove," Emil answered. "Be sure you bring it back as clean as you found it."

That afternoon, Pete ran the John Deere and a hay rack out to the north eighty. He opened a stack of alfalfa and wrestled a full rack of hay out of it. He took the load back to the barn and used the haymow fork-and-pulley system to lift the hay into the hayloft. Four fork loads transferred all the hay into the barn. Unloading hay into the loft was a two-person job. One person could do it, but it required a lot of running back and forth. He hurried to finish the hay so he could milk the cows for the second time that day. He had to pick up Chris Engelson at eight o'clock.

Pete heard the tires squeak as he backed the Studebaker out of the garage through a light covering of snow a few minutes before eight. The squeaking tires were a clue it had to be below zero. The car, kept immaculately clean by Emil, still had a faint new-car smell.

The Engelsons' yard light came on as Pete pulled the Studebaker into the driveway and stopped in front of the white two-story frame house.

Chris ambled out the door. A couple of inches taller than Pete, he moved in long easy strides, like an athlete, although he had never played any sports. Chris had unruly red hair above a long face with big ears. At nineteen, Chris had never had a girlfriend as far as Pete knew, and he wasn't surprised. Of course, Pete had never had a girlfriend either, but he didn't blame it on his looks. He thought he looked at least average, maybe a little better than average. His face wasn't as square as his dad's or as round as his mom's. Thick, crew-cut blond hair topped off a head with normal-sized ears. It wasn't that Pete didn't like girls. He spent a large part of his time thinking about them, but not knowing how to act around girls was a problem for him and for Chris, too. Neither of them had gone to high school and neither of them had any sisters. Girls were exotic creatures they didn't know much about.

Chris got into the car, and they headed for Milbank to pick up Lyle. He asked, "What's the plan for tonight?"

"Probably shoot some pool at Volk's. What you been doing this week?"

Chris replied, "I joined the marines."

The unexpected answer left Pete speechless. Finally, he exclaimed, "You what! How come?"

"You want to know the real answer?"

"Why not?"

"I got kicked out."

The answer didn't sound like the Engelsons to Pete. "I don't believe it."

"Maybe not kicked out, but they let me know in a roundabout way that I should find a way to make a living on my own. Guess I couldn't figure it out for myself. I got two younger brothers. All of us boys aren't going to be farmers. I guess I sorta knew that but didn't know what to do about it. I haven't been doing a lot of work around the farm, especially this winter. They don't need me. They don't need me around."

"Why the marines?"

"It sorta happened. Monday I took the Milwaukee train to Minneapolis. I heard factories are hiring. I wasn't too excited about a factory job, but I hafta do something."

"You took off, didn't say anything to anyone?"

"My folks knew."

"You might not have been there when I went to pick you up?"

"I've been kinda screwed up."

"You didn't finish telling me how come the marines."

"Well, I was walking down Washington Avenue, near the train depot. Not a good street, night or day. A sign in a window read: Be a Man, Join the Army. That sign got me thinking."

As they drove into Milbank, a bright moon shone on snow-covered Lake Farley on the right side of the road. Lyle lived on the lake side of the tracks in an old two-story house that backed up to Whetstone Creek. They saw Lyle looking out of the window when they pulled up.

In their threesome, Lyle was the odd one. He had lived in town all his life, in a different world. He claimed to know all about women, but Pete hadn't seen much evidence for that claim. Lyle was short compared to Pete and Chris—less than six feet by quite a bit. He had brown mouse-colored hair and a round face, with freckles over the bridge of his nose. As a counterbalance to the sober and steady Pete and Chris, Lyle compensated for his shortness by acting boisterous to the point of obnoxiousness.

Lyle trotted out of the house. "Hey, what's the plan?" he said loudly as he got into the back seat.

"Maybe some pool at Volk's," Chris replied.

Lyle faked a yawn. "That sounds exciting."

"Drink a couple of beers," Chris added.

The Studebaker idled while they discussed the evening's plans.

"Maybe we should do something special," Pete said. "With Chris going into the marines in a couple of weeks."

"What the hell are you saying?" Lyle exclaimed. "Chris is going where?"

"Marines."

"Why in hell don't I know what's going on?"

Chris explained, "I didn't know I was going into the marines last week."

Lyle wasn't buying it. "That don't make a lot of sense."

Pete reminded Chris he hadn't finished telling why he ended up in the marines.

Chris returned to his story. "Like I was telling you, I saw this sign in the window and started thinking maybe joining the army would be a better deal than working in a factory. I asked a couple of bums sitting on the curb where the army recruiting office was. They were sharing a paper sack with something in it and asked if I could spare a dollar. I gave them a quarter. They didn't have any idea where to find a recruiting office but said to try Hennepin Avenue. They said you could find most anything there. Well, I'm walking down Hennepin, and those bums were right, you could find just about anything there. Then I saw this sign on the sidewalk—you know, a tent sign, showing a marine in dress uniform holding a sword up in front of him, and I could see myself walking down Main Street in Milbank in one of those uniforms and the girls twisting their necks off looking. So I joined the marines."

"I'll be damned," Lyle said. "I guess we'll have to do something special."

Silence followed while the three young men considered their options. Finally, Lyle came up with a suggestion. "There's a dance at Chautauqua. Maybe we can get Chris screwed. Don't want to go into the marines a virgin."

Pete had never been to Chautauqua but knew enough about it to know his folks, Lutherans, who never missed church on Sunday, wouldn't approve. However, this would be one of those one-time-only occasions. Feeling a little rebellious, he seconded the idea. Chris agreed with the plan, although he had never been to Chautauqua either.

Lyle guessed that not much would happen at Chautauqua until ten at least, so he suggested a couple games of rotation at Volk's would be a good place to start.

Volk's pool hall occupied a storefront in the middle block of the town's three-block main street, a street bookended by the courthouse at the south end and the Milwaukee mainline tracks at the north end. A bar and a few tables and booths occupied the front half of the long, narrow interior, and three pool tables and a common restroom filled the back half. Being Saturday night, the front half of Volk's was filled with farmers having a beer or two while talking to other farmers about farm machinery, crops, and the weather.

After a couple of beers and two games of rotation at Volk's, Pete drove the Studebaker ten miles on Highway 12 to the town of Big Stone and another mile up Lake Road to Chautauqua Park on the shore of Big Stone Lake. The lake, thirty miles long and one mile wide, defined the border between Minnesota and South Dakota along its length. Things were jumping when they arrived, and they had to park on Lake Road, half a block from the dance hall.

"Damn, it's colder than a witch's tit!" Lyle exclaimed as they walked from the Studebaker to the dance hall. As they approached, they could hear an old-time German band pounding away. They bought their tickets, and somebody stamped the back of their hands with an ink marker.

The dance hall was a long rectangular building with a serving bar along the west side; long tables with benches that could seat eight or ten people filled three-quarters of the space. At the far end of the hall, the band played on a raised platform in front of a polished wood dance floor. The bar served only 3.2 beer but offered mixes for people who brought their own bottles.

Lyle spotted a table with some room near the dance floor and quickly claimed and held it while Pete and Chris made their way across the room. Three young women and two young men were already sitting at the table. Lyle signaled a waitress to bring them a pitcher of beer.

Lyle filled three glasses and proposed a toast. "To Chris, the best and only damn marine from Wilmot."

They emptied their glasses, and Lyle started to refill them. "No more for me," Pete said. He'd already had two beers at Volk's, and he couldn't forget he was driving his dad's nearly new car.

"Hell," Chris said, "You can't get drunk on 3.2. You'll piss it away faster than you can drink it."

Pete wasn't sure Chris's theory held water. None of the three were seasoned beer drinkers.

As though to prove his point, Chris chug-a-lugged his beer and poured another one, then held up the pitcher for a refill.

They took in their surroundings. The three women scrunched between them and the two young men at the other end of the table didn't seem to be attached to anyone. The band returned from taking a break and started playing a contemporary slow piece to get people on the floor. One of the women was asked to dance and left the table. Then the two men who had been sitting at the other end of the table stood up and started dancing with the other two women.

"What're you waiting for?" Pete asked Lyle.

"I wouldn't call them the pick of the crop. What are you two waiting for?"

"Hell, I can't dance," Pete replied. "And if I could I don't know if I would. I'm not sure I'd want to arm wrestle any of them."

Chris poured himself another beer. He agreed with Pete. "They're built like work horses."

"Nothing wrong with that," Lyle argued. "They can pitch hay all day and dance all night without working up a sweat."

They continued drinking beer and observing the dancers for a while. Chris, his voice slightly slurred, remarked, "Hell, I could do that," pointing to the dancers.

The band struck up a schottische, and most of the amateurs left the dance floor. That's when Chris persuaded one of the husky women at their table to dance.

Pete and Lyle knew this would be bad. Chris was three sheets to the wind and had never danced before, and the schottische was not a good choice to start with. The music of the schottische prompted a set pattern of steps that would have taxed Chris's abilities if he had been sober. It wasn't long before the woman attempting to dance with Chris simply walked away, leaving Chris flat-footed in the middle of the dance floor.

"Did I do good?" Chris asked when he returned to the table.

"You asshole. That pretty much messed up our chances with those women," Lyle replied.

"I did that good?" Chris replied. He hiccupped. He hiccupped again. "I know how to cure that," he murmured. He filled his glass and drank it down without taking a breath.

Pete suggested Chris take it easy.

Chris looked puzzled. "Hell, I thought we were goin' to celebrate somethin' tonight."

"We're celebrating Chris going into the marines," Pete said.

Chris looked surprised. "Chris going to the marines? Da poor bastard."

To stone-sober Pete, things at Chautauqua were visibly deteriorating. A couple of fights had broken out at the back of the room. A couple at a table across from them looked like they were about to make out. Then he noticed that Chris had disappeared. "Where's Chris?" he asked Lyle.

Lyle looked around. "Hell, he slid under the table."

"We have to get him out of here," Pete said. "I'll get the car and park it by the door."

Pete brought the Studebaker to the entrance and went inside. He and Lyle half-dragged, half-carried Chris out and dumped him in the back seat.

As they drove away from Chautauqua, Pete wondered out loud, "Now what? We can't take him home like this."

"We could set him in a snowbank," Lyle suggested. "That'd sober him up pretty quick. What time is it?"

"Little past midnight."

"The Bright Spot is the only place in Milbank open this time of the night. Maybe we can get some coffee in him."

They headed for Milbank. About halfway there, Pete heard some coughing before retching sounds erupted from the back seat. "Oh, shit, no! Lyle, what the hell is going on back there?"

"Chris just heaved all over the back seat."

"Jesus Christ!" Pete said. "My dad will kill me, actually *kill* me." He stopped the car and they dragged Chris out of the back seat, but Chris had finished doing whatever he was going to do.

Pete removed the floor coverings and wiped them clean with snow, but nothing could be done about the mess adhering to the fake mohair seat fabric.

They crammed Chris between them in the front seat and continued toward Milbank. Pete's mind churned, trying to conjure up a solution to the unsolvable problem of the messed-up back seat. As they approached the town, Chris suddenly wrapped himself around Pete, pinning his arms and completely blocking his view. Pete couldn't move his legs to step on the brake.

"Get off me, you big ass!" he shouted, trying to push Chris off.

He felt the car veering off the road. It slowly tipped and finally rolled over completely. The sound of grinding metal preceded the complete stop. The three found themselves on the car's ceiling. Pete couldn't open his door. Lyle managed to get his open and crawled out. Pete crawled over Chris, and then he and Lyle dragged Chris out. Pete observed that the beautiful Studebaker had rolled over on top of a rock pile. The front and back windows were broken out. Pete didn't investigate further. He knew the end had come. The world as he knew it had ended.

Pete asked Chris, "Can you walk?"

"Why walk?" Chris answered. "Damn cold out here."

"That's a good sign," Lyle noted. "He knows it's cold."

"Come on, let's walk," Pete said. "It's less than half a mile."

"Can somebody tell me why we are walking?" Chris asked.

"'Cause you barfed all over Pete's new car," Lyle answered, "and then wrecked it."

"Oh," Chris answered.

When the nearly frozen young men arrived at the Bright Spot, a friend of Lyle's saw them come in and greeted them. "You guys look half frozen. Car heater out?"

"Worse," Lyle replied. "Wrecked the car a ways out of town."

"Jeez, anybody hurt? Sheriff know about this?"

As far as Pete was concerned, he would prefer that nobody ever know about it. It had to be a bad dream he would wake up from any minute.

Unfortunately, Pete, still shaking from the below-zero temperature outside, knew he was wide awake. He borrowed the Bright Spot's phone and dialed the county sheriff. A sleepy Deputy David Larson answered Pete's call.

"Where did it happen?" Larson asked. "Okay, I'll drive by, take a look at it. I'll meet you at the Bright Spot, write up the report."

The young men slumped into a booth. They had gone through a pot of coffee by the time Deputy Larson showed up. Chris was asleep in a corner of the booth.

"Looks like you did a pretty good job on the Studebaker," Deputy Larson said. "Good for scrap and parts." He looked at Pete. "Want to have it towed in?"

The question surprised Pete. Like there was a choice. All the wrecks were towed into the Standard station. He didn't own the car. Maybe it didn't matter at this point. It had become a piece of junk littering a Highway 12 ditch. Pete reasoned that it would be easier to tell his dad that the car was at the Standard station than lying on its roof on top of a rock pile. At least now he wouldn't have to tell him that the back seat had been messed up. "Sure, tow it in," he said.

Deputy Larson filled out the accident report. Much of Larson's former-ly muscular body had converted to fat since he'd left the farm to become deputy sheriff five years earlier. He had bulked up into an even larger presence. The forms he filled out with a stubby pencil seemed miniature in comparison to his large, fat hand. Pete guessed that filling out accident reports wasn't one of Larson's favorite chores. There were cross-outs and inserted words; the result was a general mess. Larson pointed to where Pete needed to sign.

As he signed the form, Pete felt strange. He had never signed anything important in his life and signing an accident report that described the totaling his dad's car didn't seem like a good way to start. Deputy Larson dropped the three young men off at their homes and said he would take care of getting the car towed in the morning.

At three a.m. Pete crept up the stairs to his bedroom as quietly as possible. He got up at six a.m. as usual to feed and milk the cows. Pete had just about finished milking when Emil came in the side door of the barn.

"Where's the car?" he asked.

The moment had arrived. The world as Pete knew it would end. "The car is at the Van Dorn Standard station. I wrecked the car last night," Pete said. "Totaled it."

Emil, whose red face looked like it could explode, said, "Shit." He repeated himself. "Shit. You're a big help. Try and get ahead and you bust something. Always busting things."

Pete listened. There was some truth in what his dad said. Things did seem to break down where he was working. Last summer he was pulling a load of grain with the tractor, and somehow the load came unhitched, went in the ditch, and tipped over. A big mess. A week later he backed the pickup into the granary door. Took two days to fix the granary door, and the pickup bumper was still hanging. Then the worst—early this winter he forgot to drain the water out of the radiator after using the John Deere tractor. The water froze and busted the block.

Pete took a deep breath. "You won't have to worry about that anymore. Chris and I are joining the marines. Be leaving soon." Pete watched as the redness and angry look leaked from his dad's face.

When Pete had finally gotten to bed that morning, he laid awake, worrying about what had happened and what would happen. He couldn't imagine any good scenarios that would get him out of the mess he found himself in. It got him to thinking about another problem he had become aware of recently, the same problem Chris had. Pete had come to realize that his dream of someday farming the home place might never happen. He wasn't any closer to being a farmer than he had been five years ago when he finished the eighth grade, and he likely wouldn't be any closer five years from now.

Then a solution suddenly occurred to him. He would join the marines like Chris had done. It would diminish the current car wreck crisis by merging it with another attention-getting situation and at the same time get him out of the going-nowhere rut he was in. After resolving the matter in his mind, he fell into a deep sleep until the alarm went off at six.

Chris and Pete were inducted into the marines in Minneapolis in March 1950. A train carried them and half a dozen other marine recruits to the US Marine Corps Recruit Depot in San Diego. Pete and Chris's world view began to expand as they rode the rails in a Pullman car and ate their meals in a dining car served by Negro waiters. They saw their first mountains and deserts, plus an ocean.

A bus took the recruits from the train depot in San Diego to the training depot, where a man in a marine uniform wearing a wide-brimmed hat stepped into the bus. He started shouting, *"Listen up, recruits! You will get off this bus and plant your feet in the yellow footprints! STAND UP AND MOVE!"* There was general confusion about what and where the yellow footprints were, and Pete was thinking, there is no need to shout—we can hear you. People around Milbank didn't shout. They didn't even talk loud.

Chris must have been thinking the same thing. "Why is he shouting? Yellow footprints?"

"Shut up, shitheads!" the drill instructor yelled. *"I talk, you listen."*

Thus, the recruits were introduced to the drill instructors who would yell, curse, slap, and browbeat them for three months when the conversion of green farm boys to the earth's best fighting men would have been completed.

The recruits found the yellow footprints and stood in them. The recruits were informed about the silver doors. They would walk through the silver doors only once. When they walked through them, they would be leaving their past behind and would be where becoming marines began. As they stood at attention in the yellow footprints, they were lectured to for so long they thought they would die. Finally, they were allowed to pass through the silver doors.

As farm boys, Pete and Chris were used to physical activity. They found that part of the training challenging but nothing they couldn't handle. But as young men raised in a culture of independent thinking, other aspects of training took some getting used to, such as obeying without question the commands of superiors. One example of this was the close-order drill, in which a platoon is trained to act as one. However, by the end of three months the drill instructors had worked their magic. At the graduation ceremonies, each company of recruits marched like a well-oiled machine.

Upon graduation from recruit training, Pete and Chris were given a twenty-day furlough, with orders to report to the First Marine Division stationed at Camp Pendleton upon return.

They chose the bus as the most economical way to travel to their homes in South Dakota, where they would meet anxious parents and enjoy home cooking for a while.

Although they didn't wear the blue marine dress uniform in Milbank—Pete said he would feel like a peacock in it—they attracted considerable attention by wearing the less formal marine green trousers and khaki shirts with ties. The town was proud to have these tall young marines as members of the community.

Pete and Chris agreed to observe their traditional Saturday night get-together with Lyle on the last Saturday before they returned to California. They thought they should do something special. After considerable discussion and shared doubts, they decided to repeat the disastrous Chautauqua visit but do it right this time. They were successful in that Chris did not demonstrate that one cannot get drunk on 3.2 beer and the women sharing their table didn't reject them. The Chautauqua retake was pronounced a success.

Pete turned on the radio as they drove back to Milbank, and the song "Harbor Lights" emanated from the speaker. Pete's folks had replaced the wrecked Studebaker with a new one and he was surprised they let him drive it. The prodigal son had apparently been forgiven. A voice broke through the music and announced, "WCCO radio is interrupting this program to bring you breaking news. An Associated Press report confirms that at dawn Sunday, the twenty-fifth of June, elements of the North Korean Army crossed the border into South Korea, and it appears that a full-scale invasion of the south by the north is occurring. Stay tuned for further developments." WCCO switched back to normal programming, and the sounds of "Mona Lisa" drifted into the Studebaker.

"What the fuck?" Chris exclaimed. "Where is Korea?"

Pete had a pretty good idea where things were in East Asia. "Hangs off northern China," he replied with an air of certainty.

"Okay," Chris said. "I remember now. You think we'll get involved?" he asked in a manner that sounded like he knew the answer.

Lyle didn't think so. "Can't be very important if I never heard of the place."

"Because you don't know shit about Korea doesn't mean it isn't important," Chris declared.

Pete followed current events closely, like other people followed sports. "It isn't about Korea," Pete said. "It's about communism. North Korea is communist and South Korea isn't. That's why it's important."

"Don't like what I'm hearing," Chris said. "This isn't in the plan."

"What plan?" Pete asked.

"Our marine enlistment plans. It's about seeing the world and meeting some wild women, nothing about war."

"Never told me about any plan," Pete said.

"Not on paper," Chris replied. "But that's what I've been thinking. No war in the plan."

Lyle chimed in. "Sounds like you need to update your plan."

"Don't get too smug, Lyle," Pete said. "They could crank up the draft again."

"You think so?" Lyle asked. "They wouldn't."

"You can beat that. Join the marines," Chris suggested.

"That sounds like shooting yourself in the head to save your foot," Lyle replied. "No thanks."

After the chatter died down, the young marines worked the unexpected news over in their minds. Things out of Pete and Chris's control were happening that could affect their lives in a bad way. This wouldn't be something Pete and Chris would read about; it would be happening to them.

The next day, Sunday, June 25, the Houser family went to church. His mother insisted Pete wear his uniform. "You look so good when you wear it," she said.

Pete had not said anything about the news he heard the night before, and since his folks hadn't mentioned Korea, he assumed they hadn't heard anything. They were walking from their parked car to the church when Ralph Shuman, a neighbor who lived south of their place, asked them what they thought about the Korean news.

"What news?" Pete's dad asked.

Shuman replied, "Something about the north invading the south. It's all over the news."

They listened to the car radio while driving home after church. Korea dominated the news. There were emergency meetings in Washington, and the United Nations would meet on Monday to discuss the crisis.

"What's this all about?" Pete's mother wanted to know.

"Just hope we don't get involved," Pete's dad declared. "Let 'em fight. Who cares?"

From what Pete heard on the radio, it seemed clear that the United States would become involved. It wasn't being described as a war between two parts of a small divided country; rather it was part of a bigger picture, a part of the Red Tide, the communist threat to the free world.

Pete's mother didn't seem concerned about the big picture. She was concerned about how it would affect her boy. "Will you have to go to Korea?" she asked Pete.

"Don't know," Pete replied. But privately he believed that if the United States did get involved, the First Marine Division would be ripe for participating.

Pete and Chris got together Sunday afternoon. Korea dominated their thoughts. By this time, they had little doubt that Korea would involve Marine Corps participation.

"Marines will lead the charge," Chris mused. "Guess it's what we trained for. War and killing people.

On June 29, President Harry S. Truman ordered a naval blockade of the Korean coast and authorized General Douglas A. MacArthur to send US ground troops into Korea. General MacArthur began moving army troops stationed in Japan to South Korea and requested of the Joint Chiefs of Staff that a marine regimental combat team be deployed to the Far East.

These events answered any questions in Chris and Pete's minds with regards to how the United States would respond to the invasion of South Korea.

When it was time for Chris and Pete to return to California, they and their families waited outside of the drug store where the Greyhound bus would stop to pick up passengers. When they'd left for boot camp, only Pete's mother had been there to send them off. This time, current events drew everyone in their immediate families to the departure. Although not discussed openly, the possibility of these young men going halfway around the world to face unknown dangers weighed heavily on these families. Pete's mother, who had become emotional when they were leaving for boot camp, hugged Pete long and warmly but remained stoic during the sendoff, as if to demonstrate strength during a crisis. Even Pete's dad moved outside his comfort zone and gave Pete a warm hug.

When Pete and Chris arrived at Camp Pendleton Marine Base in California to report in at the Marine First Division, they were directed to a place where the First Provisional Marine Brigade was being formed in response to General Douglas MacArthur's request that a marine regimental team be sent to Korea as soon as possible.

The two South Dakota farm boys who had just recently been pronounced marines when they graduated from the Marine Corps Training Center in California realized they were on a fast track to go to war. What had seemed only a possibility was now reality. Each of them absorbed the information and processed it in his own individual way.

It made Pete's whole body feel strange for a moment, as if the news had affected his whole being and it was reorganizing itself to adapt. Like one life had ended and a new one was beginning.

Chris used to enjoy watching the war newsreels that were shown before a movie. Now he felt like he was in one of those war news films. In a way it was scary and, in a way, exciting. Now the First Marine Brigade would be in the news, and the people in Milbank would be watching it.

The brigade quickly organized. Pete and Chris ended up partnered on a fire team, Chris the Browning Automatic Rifle (BAR) man with Pete as his assistant. The fire team was part of a squad that consisted of four fire teams and a squad leader. Their fire team leader was Corporal Brad Hautman, a World War II veteran, and their rifleman was Adam Anderson, a farm boy from North Dakota and a recent recruit. They were the First Fire Team in the Second Squad in the First Platoon, Easy Company, in the Fifth Battalion. Within days the First Marine Brigade was loading onto ships at San Diego Navy Base and departing for Korea.

The brigade quickly unloaded upon docking at the port of Pusan and joined the United Nations (UN) coalition, fighting to maintain the Pusan Perimeter, the last tenuous foothold left on the Korean Peninsula.

Pete and Chris soon learned that war for an infantryman entailed more than fear and excitement. The lot of the infantryman at war has not changed fundamentally since time immemorial. It involves imminent contact with the enemy, terribly dirty conditions, sleeping on the ground or in holes in the ground, eating cold rations, and lots of spilled blood, human suffering, and death.

Most men who serve as infantrymen adapt; some don't. Those that do normalize their existence. They form a close bond with those who share their experience.

After five weeks of almost constant combat and substantial losses, the First Marine Brigade was pulled back and retrofitted, their losses replaced. The First Fire Team suffered only minor wounds in all the action. Pete's back was peppered with grenade shrapnel, and Corporal Hautman, the fire team leader, had a bullet pass through his helmet and graze his forehead. In both cases the minor wounds were treated with first aid.

Most of the marines thought they would be put back in the line after some rest, but instead the brigade and its men and equipment were put on ships and seagoing landing craft. The First Marine Brigade ships joined a large convoy of other ships and landing craft carrying the First Marine Division and the Army Seventh Infantry Division. The marines in the First Provisional Marine Brigade found out that they were now part of the First Marine Division and that they would be making an amphibious landing at a place called Inchon.

The landing at Inchon took the North Korean enemy completely by surprise. After a few days of sometimes intense fighting, Seoul, the capital of South Korea, was occupied by Allied troops.

Once Seoul was secured, the First Marine Division moved back to Inchon, where it was again retrofitted, and lost men replaced. It soon became known that the First Marine Division would again be loading onto ships and making another amphibious landing. Where that would be was unknown.

On October 15, 1950, the convoy carrying the First Marine Division to its next destination set sail. What was supposed to be a three-day sail to Wonsan on the North Korean east coast turned into an eleven-day back and forth in the Sea of Japan while unexpected mines were cleared from the Wonsan harbor. In the meantime, Wonsan was occupied by UN forces traveling overland.

After the inauspicious start, the First Marine Division and other UN forces began moving into the Taebaek Mountains on a primitive mountain trail hardly wide enough for ox carts to pass. Even the men in the First Fire Team suspected it was not a good tactic to string out a marine division and other UN forces on this mountain trail that hardly deserved to be called a road. There were no alternative ways to get to or from the trail from anywhere else. All the supplies for over thirty-five thousand men and their equipment would have to move on this road.

The First Fire Team and some of the other members of the squad discussed the situation. Pete suggested that the Inchon landing had been so successful General Douglas MacArthur thought he was God.

Pete continued, "MacArthur is in his Tokyo office looking at a map and sees this road running from the coast and through the mountains almost straight north to the Yalu River and the China border. So, MacArthur says, 'We'll just have some marines drive up that road and occupy that part of the border.'"

Sarcasm is a common trait among men involved in combat for long periods, and there was no shortage of it in Easy Company, First Platoon, Fifth Battalion, men who had fought in the Pusan Perimeter and Inchon landing before entering the tenuous trail.

Marine General Oliver led the First Marine Division and apparently had similar concerns as the men in the First Platoon, Easy Company. He had his orders to advance along this mountain road to the Yalu River. He was following orders but slow-walked the division's advance along the mountain road. He assigned men to guard their flanks along the roadside. He built supply depots in villages along the path of the advance, occupied them, and built defense perimeters around them. He had two air strips bulldozed out of the frozen terrain.

Although North Korean forces had evaporated for the most part, there were rumors and concerns about the Chinese entering the war. The further the marines advanced into the mountains, the more obvious the Chinese threat became. At one point there was a pitched battle between a marine regiment and a large force identified as Chinese. Soon they were seeing more signs of the Chinese presence and seeing figures in quilted jackets in the distance on a regular basis. Patrols moving out from the perimeters were skirmishing with Chinese patrols. Still the orders remained to advance toward their objective.

Another enemy was the weather. The marines had been advancing during the month of November; winter was firmly established in the Taebaek Mountains. The marines had advanced sixty miles and occupied a village called Hagaru near the Chosin Reservoir. By this time, they were experiencing temperatures as low as twenty below zero. Pete and Chris had grown up in South Dakota and had seen weather twenty below and colder but had never lived in it twenty-four hours a day while they had to sleep in fox holes. Weapons wouldn't fire; trucks wouldn't start. Frostbite became a common occurrence. Rations froze.

After spending an extended period of time at Hagaru, the First Fire Team had begun to feel at home, despite the worsening weather and the almost daily patrols outside of their perimeter. That changed on Thanksgiving Day, when they were told the Fifth Regiment would be moving up the mountain road fourteen more miles to another small village called Yudam-ni.

When the Fifth Regiment arrived in Yudam-ni, the First Fire Team learned that the regiment would be leading a diversion the next morning, advancing over a primitive mountain road to the west to link up with the Eighth Army advancing to the east.

The advance started the next morning and soon ran into stiff resistance from Chinese, who were dug into the hills in line with the advance. The Fifth Regiment made little progress and dug in for the night, planning to continue in the morning.

The temperature dropped to twenty-five degrees below zero. Chinese began probing the Easy Company line. Everyone in the First Fire Team was awake. Ominous feelings ran through the First Fire Team members. Bugles and whistles began sounding down the slope from where Easy Company had established their line of defense. A mortar flare lit up the area. Pete and Chris peered at the scene below. Masses of men were advancing in orderly columns up the slope, headed for their line of fox holes. Everything in the line began firing at the masses advancing toward them—machine guns, M1 rifles, and BARs such as Pete and Chris used started to pump out lead. Mortars began dropping rounds on the columns. The withering fire stalled the lead columns and they evaporated, but other columns kept advancing and began to overrun the line of fox holes. Reserves filled holes in the line, and eventually the attack was stalled. The Chinese fell back. The first light of a new day appeared. The attack was over. Corsair fighter planes appeared and began attacking any visible surviving enemies.

The gruesome work of locating wounded marines needing care and locating and removing the dead began. Among the dead were Pete and Chris in their foxhole, Chris still gripping his BAR weapon and Pete holding a clip of ammunition in his hand, ready to slam it into the BAR when needed.

The Fifth Regiment was not the only unit under attack that night. Every unit defending the perimeter that ran for miles in hills surrounding the Yudam-ni plateau had been attacked. The Chinese had the best fighting elements of the First Marine Division in their trap and were now going to kill them. The Chinese had put twelve divisions into the Chosin Reservoir area with the mission to destroy the Marine First Division. The marines at Yudam-ni and those strung along the mountain road along which they had advanced had a different plan. They would fight their way out of the trap. Marine General Oliver summed it up: "We're not retreating, we're attacking in a new direction."

The seven-day battle in which the marines fought their way back down the primitive mountain road to the sea with all their equipment has become an epic chapter in United States Marine history.

They were not able to bring out all the dead. They had difficulty finding transport to bring out the wounded in the advance to the sea, so most of the dead were buried in mass graves at sites along the mountain road. Pete and Chris were buried along with other marines killed at Yudam-ni in a mass grave before the marines fought their way out of that valley.

On a cold February day, people who lived in and near Milbank, South Dakota, gathered in the city auditorium to honor Peter Houser and Chris Engelson, local sons and heroes who died for their country in a cold and desolate faraway place. Lyle Houser, close friend of Pete and Chris, was among those in the auditorium. Next to the immediate families, Lyle felt the loss of his good friends as much as anyone. As Lyle listened to the words praising Pete and Chris for their patriotism, bravery, and sacrifice, he questioned the accuracy of some of what was being said. He didn't question that they were brave and had sacrificed their lives but did question the notion that patriotism was what drove them to enlist in the marines. Lyle, being aware of what had led them to join the marines, knew that it had little, if anything, to do with patriotism or willingness to sacrifice their lives for flag or country. Pete and Chris had no intention of becoming heroes. For Pete and Chris, the Marine Corps provided what they believed to be an opportunity to move into the next phase of their lives. They were focused on their future, not the country's future. However, despite their original intent, they had become unintended heroes and sacrificed their lives for their country. That was reality, and Lyle did not question that.

Moon Shot

MAN ON THE MOON

Photograph is in the public domain

Moon Shot

The Cold War was at its peak when President Kennedy first broached the idea of sending a man to the moon in a speech to a joint congressional audience in May 1961. Part of the Cold War competition involved developing a superior capability in space. Putting a man on the moon would be a dramatic demonstration of the United States capabilities. The idea had bipartisan congressional support, and money was appropriated to explore the feasibility of the idea and develop a plan to land men on the moon and return them safely to earth.

The United States industrial complex took immediate notice of the possibility of lucrative government contracts. No company could claim experience in landing a man on the moon, but any company that had ever gotten near a rocket or launch site, and some that never had, was eager to pitch their capabilities to lead or assist in an effort to land a man on the moon.

In 1962 the president was able to announce in Houston, the city where the national space center would be located, the plan to develop the capability to fly men to the moon and return them to the earth by the end of the decade.

Companies sniffing out the moon landing contract possibilities included Data Action Corporation (DAC), Government Systems Division, located in Minneapolis, Minnesota. DAC Government Systems management asked their Washington marketing people to beat the bushes for opportunities related to the moon landing program.

The Washington DAC sales office had been recently put together and was thin in experience and contacts, particularly with regards to NASA. The fledgling company had never worked on any NASA contracts. The DAC salesperson eventually selected to lead the DAC effort was a hillbilly from the hills of Tennessee named Dan Daggart. Dan, like the other people in the office, had no previous experience with NASA programs or contacts with people in the NASA orbit. However, the other leads Dan had for DAC opportunities had turned out to be dry holes and he was looking for something to do. So, he became the logical choice to check out NASA possibilities.

Dan had been hired recently. His resume indicated he had been knocking around Washington for a while, working mostly for tech companies and pitching equipment and services to federal agencies or prime contractors for use in military programs.

Dan's parents were tobacco farmers, with moonshine as a sideline. Dan wasn't interested in the tobacco part of the family business but considered moonshine as a future. He changed his mind about the business when his parents got busted. He decided to explore other options. Despite the difficulties the parents were experiencing, the family moonshine business had provided a substantial sum of assets safely hidden from federal agent eyes that Dan could tap. Surprisingly, Dan decided to use some of those funds for educational purposes and enrolled in a local college. He didn't know what he wanted to study but wanted it to be something useful. His student advisor suggested something to do with technology would be good. However, the only thing close to technology the college offered was general science. So Dan got a BA in General Science and went to Washington to find a job.

Dan had a way with people and made friends easily. Women seemed attracted to Dan, although it wasn't obvious why. Physically Dan was on the short side, five-feet-seven inches tall, of average build, with receding straight black hair. However, he had a gift of gab and a southern drawl that put women at ease on first contact.

Back in Minneapolis, a group in the DAC Government Systems Division was designated as Marketing Support. It was made up mostly of engineers who found their expertise was not in design, analysis, documenting, or troubleshooting of inanimate objects but more in the people-to-people interaction that goes on with any human activity. Other engineers who were especially creative and productive were promoted out of work they liked and put into Marketing Support, where they were often a poor fit. And there always seemed to be few misfits gaming the system in Marketing Support, talking the talk but faking their level of expertise.

As a starting point in getting his arms around the NASA market, Dan decided to contact DAC Marketing Support in Minneapolis to see what they knew about NASA. What he learned wasn't promising. But Bert Johansson, manager of DAC Government Systems Marketing Support, thought that a person who spent most of his time in the Washington office might have some ideas about NASA. His name was John Forsum.

John Forsum was a Minneapolis native whose family had the means to support numerous city's amenities related to the arts and music. John's father was a lawyer associated with a prestigious law firm and, since John had been a good student, had encouraged him to pursue a prestigious profession such as law or medicine. Cost was not a concern.

Though he had the ability and means to pursue his father's suggestions, John was put off by the effort needed to accomplish what was suggested. However, it was a given that he would go to college. He attended the University of Minnesota and earned a BA in history. He took part in the Navy ROTC program at the university and after graduating took flight training at Pensacola, flying F9F fighters during his active-duty obligation. The navy service and family connections got John a job with DAC in Government Systems Marketing Support.

John spent much of his time in Washington and had appropriated an unused space in the DAC Washington office for his own use. John had a way of working the system for his own benefit.

John had a wife and two children who didn't see much of him since he spent so much time in Washington. He was a people person and enjoyed entertaining customers visiting Minneapolis or when he visited out-of-town customers. His wife didn't complain but had mentioned at times and in different ways that she wished he didn't have to work so hard and could spend more time with the family. John considered himself to be a good provider and felt that satisfied his primary family obligation.

Dan found John Forsum ensconced in a small office outside of the DAC Government Systems office area in a larger DAC Commercial Systems Marketing area in the building. They introduced themselves. John explained his isolated office space. "My real office is in Minneapolis, but most of my business is in Washington, so I appropriated this office."

"Per diem expenses paid?" Dan asked.

"Of course," John replied.

"What a deal!" The two of them took an immediate liking to each other.

Dan explained why he had come looking for John. "John, I'm looking for somebody in our organization who knows something about NASA or has contacts in NASA. No luck so far. They tell me Government Systems hasn't done any business with NASA but said I should talk to John Forsum anyway."

John laughed. "That sounds like a hell of a recommendation."

Dan agreed. "That's what I thought, but here I am."

They talked about life in general for a while before John returned to the subject at hand. "I'm thinking," he said, "of an old drinking buddy I knew when I was in the navy. I flew wing with him in Korea. Pete Winter—he was crazy. I haven't kept in contact with him, but I understand he has risen to a level of some importance in NASA. Might be worth a try."

Dan laughed. "I would call that a shot in the dark, not a contact. I'm assuming you'll get right on it."

John located his old wing mate. Not too hard to do if the person you're looking for is on an upper level in the NASA command structure. Pete's office was in Houston, where the space center was being built, but he visited Washington regularly. They agreed to meet the following week, when Pete would be in Washington. They met at a favorite restaurant for contractors and government people procuring items for the military or NASA programs. It was expensive, a plus for the government people since the contractors always picked up the check. They had a substantial lunch and a drink or two and talked about life on a carrier and their favorite liberty ports. Eventually John moved the discussion to the moon landing and what part Pete was playing in the program.

"My concern is prelaunch checkout," Pete replied. "Making sure everything is working before we launch."

"Sounds like a good idea. After launch it's a little late to find a problem. What you guys are attempting seems out of this world. A lot of people, including myself, wonder if this is possible. I know you have that big rocket, the Atlas, but I don't think you will be landing it on the moon."

"Some physicists at Redstone have come up with the way it's going to be done," Pete replied. "When I heard how they were planning to do it, my first reaction was there is no way that will work. NASA has put together an animation that shows how it is to be done. They say it isn't just the best way to do it, it's the only way to do it. It looks scarier than flying an F9 off a carrier. A spacecraft that will carry three people with hardly space for two will fly to the moon and then orbit around it. This spacecraft has a moon lander attached to it. While the spacecraft orbits the moon, the lander with two astronauts in it will be detached and descend and land on the moon. After they land, they will look around and walk around for a while and plant a flag. Then they get back in their lander, take off, and rendezvous with the orbiting spacecraft, which then returns to earth. They splash down somewhere in the Pacific Ocean, where they hope somebody will pick them up."

"What are the odds of that happening?" John asked. "Don't know if I would trust those physicists if I was an astronaut. Imagine being in that lander. Say you bang up the lander, can't take off. You're done. Nobody you can call for help. Maybe you do get off the moon and then can't connect with the spacecraft. Nobody has ever done that for real before."

Pete agreed. "But the physicists say they have the math that proves that it can be done the way they are describing it. Astronauts are lining up and clamoring to make the trip. Go figure. Humans are weird animals."

"Anyway," John said, "I'm not here to criticize the Redstone physicists. I'm here to see if there is anything the company I represent can contribute to this crazy plan."

"For starters," Pete said, "wherever possible, we are looking for off-the-shelf hardware that can do the job. Space used to be about the future. The moon shot is about today. It has to be done with today's technology. Main reason for that is we have to beat the Russians, so there's no time to invent new things. We are going to use off-the-shelf components as much as possible."

John asked, "You going to use off-the-shelf computers?"

"Everything is on the table," Pete replied. "Computers are key to an automated pre-launch checkout system. We would like to find one that can do the job. At the same time, we don't want to compromise. That computer and every other component in the checkout system must be as good as we can make it. We want to ensure everything is working perfectly on that bird when it's launched."

John guessed the astronauts would second that idea. "Who is looking for these off-the-shelf components?" he asked.

Pete said, "NASA's Preflight Operations, located in Daytona, is scouring the country for off-the-shelf components, computers being one of them." He volunteered to look up who John needed to contact in Preflight to discuss computers.

John felt like he had hit a home run when he left the meeting. Optimism was a necessary characteristic for anyone marketing to the federal government's military and space markets; otherwise it could be a career full of disappointments. John had been doing all right during the six years he'd been at DAC. He had participated in putting together proposal after proposal. Small ones, big ones, proposals they should have won, proposals they shouldn't have bid on, and some that they won. However, he had not won a big one, one that could keep Government Systems busy for years and lead to other NASA contracts. John believed the moon program could be a big win, and winning a big one was what every marketing person in the business hoped for, the kind that could keep the Government Systems Division in business for years and, as a side benefit, keep John employed.

Pete gave John Ben Hauge's name in Preflight Operations, and John passed the information to Dan Daggart, who contacted Ben. Ben had a loud, intimidating telephone voice but sounded interested in having DAC describe how they could satisfy the computer requirements.

Dan mentioned the DAC6A as a possibility. Ben had heard about the computer and said they were using it in the Gemini program.

Technical details weren't Dan's strength, but he knew some of the highlights of the DAC6A. Dan described it as a mini computer that, although small, could run FORTRAN, so it was pretty capable. Dan asked if NASA had documented the requirements for the computer they were looking for.

"We have," Ben replied. "They are in a state of flux but should be good enough to figure out what the computer has to do. I'll send you a copy. What kind of price we talking about for the DAC6A?"

"The basic unit is about fifty thousand dollars," Dan replied.

Ben sounded surprised. "That's interesting," he said.

They agreed to meet in Daytona in January 1962 so DAC could pitch their computer solution.

John and Dan huddled. They needed a budget, and they needed technical people who knew something about computers. John and Dan could recognize a computer if they saw one, but that was about the level of their knowledge on the subject.

John planned to work on lining up the technical people they would need. Dan would come to Minneapolis, despite the approaching winter, to help obtain the funds they'd need to pursue the opportunity.

John talked to Max Heimer, manager of Government Systems Design, about support for the NASA opportunity.

"This another one of your wild goose chases?" Max asked.

John and Max had worked together often, and their communications were informal, direct, and unfiltered.

"I'm going to win a contract so you can keep your job." John replied. "I'll need some of your best people for this job."

Max wasn't impressed. "Show me what we need to do, and I'll tell you who we have available to work on it."

John handed Max a copy of the draft computer requirements that NASA's Ben Hauge had sent to Dan Daggart.

"You got a charge number?" Max asked.

"Charge overhead while I get a number approved."

"Easier to get a proposal number than charge to overhead."

"Jeez, how many hours do you need? We mentioned the DAC6A as a candidate, the only thing we could think of. While you are eating your lunch, scan the requirements and figure out if the DAC6A can do the job. If it can't, then we'll have figure out what we have to do to make the DAC6 able to do the job or find something else that will work."

"Okay. Means I'll miss playing duplicate bridge during lunch. You'll owe me."

"Like I said, I'll get us a contract so you can keep your job."

The next morning, John checked with Max to see what he had learned about the requirements.

Max sat in his office drinking his first cup of coffee from the department party-sized percolator. Max was and looked like a consummate engineer: in need of a haircut, wearing horn-rim glasses, a tie with minor food stains, a pocket protector with two number-two pencils and a six-inch slide rule. He looked slightly malnourished and seemed to look past you when he talked to you.

He greeted John. "Hell, I was wasting my time. If you had read a page or two of the requirements, even you could have figured out the DAC6A wouldn't cut it."

"True, but I had to get an expert opinion."

"Okay. So if you are serious about this, you will have to bring a logic guy and a programmer in, plus a memory guy and a guy to concentrate on the input-output peripherals. Oh, and a mechanical guy. Everything will have to be repackaged. Even the cabinet colors need to be coordinated with the rest of the preflight checkout system. You can save the components—most circuit boards are off-the-shelf—and memory modules design will have to be modified. All of the logic for the computer, memory and input out modules will be original design. Everything else has to be put together in a different way. What I'm describing is what we need to invent in order to meet NASA's requirements. Then calculate the nonrecurring and recurring costs to put together a prototype and fourteen acceptance checkout equipment production computer systems. Don't know if division management will spend that kind of money on something they have never heard about before. It might be some NASA engineer's wet dream. Oh, I would guess the twelve-bit word the DAC6A uses isn't going to work because there may not be enough bits in the word for all of the new instructions."

"Sounds like you are designing something from scratch. Where does the DAC6A fit in?" John asked.

"Maybe we can save the logo—not much else. They are asking for complete redundancy between two main frames with remote memories shared by both computers and two redundant input-output modules with redundant peripherals shared by both computer systems. It's quite a maze. They describe an interrupt system that sounds like a jig saw puzzle. We need sixteen-thousand-byte core memories in the computer main frames and double that in the remote memory modules. This is not a DAC6A."

"How in hell are we going to sell something like you describe as off-the-shelf?"

"Want my take on this off-the-shelf thing?" Max asked. He then proceeded without an answer to his question. "Well, somebody up there, way up there, decided they could save a lot of money and time if they got all the stuff they needed to check the rocket, the space capsule, and the moon lander with off-the-shelf equipment. Just hook all those off-the-shelf things together and turn the power on. At the same time, some engineers down at the bottom, way down at the bottom, are figuring out the details of how to check out this spacecraft and everything associated with it to make sure it is working perfectly before it blasts off for the moon. Those engineers don't care how the hardware to do this is procured. They just care that it's able to do what it has to do."

"Okay," John said. "So how does that solve the off-the-shelf problem for us?"

"That's your part to figure out," Max replied. "One thing I can assure you is that our competition hasn't anything off-the-shelf that can meet those requirements either."

John met Dan when he arrived to help sell the program to division management. He informed Dan that things were becoming a little complicated.

"How's that?" Dan asked.

"The NASA computer requirements and DAC6A have nothing in common," John replied.

"Sounds like we will hafta earn our pay," Dan said. "It'll probably be easier to sell this to NASA than the front office."

"What are we going to sell?" John wanted to know.

"Whatever meets NASA's requirements," Dan replied. "Maybe we should call it something different than DAC6A if it's a different machine."

They mulled that over for a while. John thought they should keep the DAC6 part of the name so it sounded more off-the-shelf. Dan agreed. They named it the DAC6G, the "G" denoting its Government Systems connection.

Management did authorize the money to configure a system to meet the NASA's computer requirements and to cost it out. The proposal crew worked over the holidays to nail down the design concepts. They decided that they needed an extra bit in the computer word size to accommodate the instruction set. They used the circuit components and many of the circuit boards in the DAC6A. Several new circuit boards needed to be developed. The memory modules had to be redesigned to accommodate the thirteen-bit word. New software to test and verify the new computer design was required. The biggest cost item was the logic design needed to make the hardware perform as needed. And finally, everything had to be repackaged to meet NASA's requirement for standard cabinet design.

The cost estimates came together; marketing and program managers battled with production and engineering managers to keep the costs down. The recurring price to NASA for an ACE computer system came in at approximately two hundred thousand dollars with normal markups, no development costs included.

John and Dan worked the NASA connections they had and determined that NASA had budgeted about half what Government Systems estimated the recurring cost would be. They also determined that many of the budget estimates for the moon landing program were derived by throwing numbers at a wall; if they stuck, NASA used them. So, numbers were flexible. They banked on Max Heimer's guess that meeting the requirements was more important than NASA cost estimates.

John and Dan were confident the numbers Government Systems had produced were reasonable and justifiable for what NASA was asking for. The numbers had been massaged as much as they could be. To manufacture something that met NASA's requirements would cost NASA two hundred thousand dollars, not including development costs.

Again, based on what they could find out from NASA contacts and their gut feelings, John and Dan concluded NASA would pay the development costs for the stand-alone memory and I/O modules. However, NASA would assume they were receiving a modified DAC6A computer as the main frame for the ACE computer system and would not pay directly for any of its development cost—despite the fact that nothing resembling what was being proposed had ever been built before.

Development costs for the main frame computer were estimated at a million dollars. Marketing gurus John Forsum and Dan Daggart had a million-dollar problem.

They decided they should plan a long lunch at one of the 494 watering holes to help concentrate their thinking. They invited Max Heimer, the design manager, to join them, but he declined, opting to play duplicate bridge during lunch.

They started on their second martinis before confronting their problem.

John mentioned that the two main frame computers in each system would make the problem a little easier.

Dan agreed. "How many times does twenty-eight go into a million? I was never any good at math."

John got out a pen, made the calculation on a napkin. "It's a big number—about thirty-seven thousand times."

Dan said, "You know what we have to do. We need to have a bigger number in the denominator. We need to sell this computer to more customers."

John had been down this road before but not in the direct line of fire. "Government Systems isn't in that line of business. Government Systems doesn't invest company money to develop products. The last people who tried that aren't around anymore. Besides, this is a commercial product. We aren't in that market."

The martinis were slowing down Dan's thinking. Finally, he asked John, "What do we get if we divide the million by fifty?"

John, apparently still alert, rebounded with, "Twenty thousand," without making the calculation.

"That's the number we will use," Dan declared.

"Didn't you hear me?" John asked. "We don't do that kind of thing in Government Systems."

Dan, who apparently wasn't paying attention, replied, "We'll have Commercial put it in their catalog."

John wanted to believe Dan. He wanted to believe that Max Heimer and his crew had come up with something that could be sold despite Government Systems' past failures to do similar things. Despite his doubts he began exploring the path Dan was leading them down.

John pointed out that even if they did what Dan was suggesting, they would exceed the target price of two hundred thousand dollars.

"But by less," Dan replied. "It could be manageable. We could massage the numbers some more. Management could take less net, maybe exceed the target by, say, five thousand."

John pointed out that in the real world, management wouldn't gamble a half a million dollars to win this contract. "They aren't that dumb or desperate."

"I'm not sure about the last part of what you just said," Dan replied. "They are in pretty bad need of some new business. I move we amortize the DAC6G nonrecurring costs over fifty units and see where the chips fall."

John didn't agree, but his mind was burdened by the three martinis he'd recently consumed. He couldn't come up with anything better than Dan was proposing.

"Remember," Dan said, "we are in this together. We are going to convince management to do what they need to do to win this contract."

John wasn't focused on what Dan was saying. He was thinking about what he would do when he was fired.

Before leaving the restaurant, John sketched their plan on a napkin. "Never going to remember what we talked about when we get back to the office."

DAC Government Systems Division was headed by a general manager named Robert Glassman, who had held that position for a little over a year. The tenure of general managers in the Government Systems Division had a tendency to be short lived. Competition for government contracts in the defense and technology business was brutal. Government Systems Division general managers were expected to grow the business and profits in that competitive market. Historically, general managers had been able to grow the business or the profits but not both simultaneously. Bidding low might grow the business but hurt profits, while maintaining profits might cost the business growth.

Glassman felt confident enough that he could be successful that he had moved his family from Boston to the Twin Cities and bought a home in a tony suburb—in spite of the fact that Glassman had already moved his family half a dozen times while moving from company to company. During that process, he had moved up from engineer to division management level in the last two companies where he had worked. That was a very vulnerable management level, with high casualties when numbers upper management wanted were missed.

The pressure of the job had left its marks on Robert Glassman. In his fifties, he was prematurely gray, smoked heavily, and had not tried to remain physically fit and succeeded. However, he maintained a dominating presence in the space he occupied. Managing was his natural habitat and where he wanted to be.

Glassman had been kept informed of the ACE opportunity and the latest developments, as had the staff that would be approving the design and cost estimates. Glassman had a computer background and understood that the redundant capabilities being proposed would provide computer system reliability not previously feasible.

Goldman and his staff gathered in early January to review the final design and prices the division had worked up to present to NASA in Daytona the following week.

Max Heimer, system design manager, presented the final design information. Max had become enamored with what his design team had come up with, and it showed in his presentation. It was a system he would like to see built.

Glassman and staff didn't ask a lot of questions about the design or capabilities of the computer and seemed satisfied with what they were shown.

John Forsum delivered the cost and price part of the presentation. The first item projected on the screen was a recurring price for an ACE computer system of 212,000 dollars.

John and Dan had hoped to squeeze more cost out of operations, but the costs had been squeezed to the point where there was no squeeze left. Program Management cut an assistant and contributed a three-thousand-dollar reduction to the recurring cost. They arbitrarily reduced the fee by five thousand dollars to cut the recurring price down to 212,000 dollars, which didn't raise any alarms from management; nor did exceeding the original price goal by twelve thousand dollars raise any questions. The nonrecurring development cost for the external memory and I/O units were included in the bid as expected. However, the development cost for the DAC6G mainframe didn't show up anywhere.

"Did you forget something?" Glassman asked, "The cost of the mainframe. That has to be a big chunk of it."

John explained to Glassman and his staff that NASA expected the DAC6G to be off-the-shelf and to not have to pay for the development of that aspect of the ACE system. Therefore, the estimated million-dollar development cost of the DAC6G would be amortized at twenty thousand dollars per unit sold over fifty units.

At that point in the presentation, a stunned look appeared on Glassman's face, and the staff exchanged surprised looks.

"Why?" Glassman asked. "Why is the DAC6G development being amortized over fifty units? I believe NASA is buying fourteen production systems."

John explained that there were two DAC6G computers in each ACE system, for a total of twenty-eight computers and that NASA was looking for off-the-shelf hardware where possible; the DAC6G had been promoted as off-the-shelf. Marketing was projecting that other military, NASA, and commercial applications would make the DAC6G a contender for systems needing high fail-safe reliability.

"When did twenty-eight become fifty?" Glassman asked.

Once again, John explained, "NASA is expecting the DAC6G to be off-the-shelf, and if we include all of the nonrecurring costs in the DAC6G price we will not be competitive."

"Who is we?" Glassman asked.

The question made John realize that the "we" had been Dan and himself. They had been doing the NASA briefings and planting the idea that the "G" version of the DAC6 was off-the-shelf.

"Well, a lot of people" John replied.

"Be more specific. I'd like to know who I need to fire."

John felt like he was taking part in a circular firing squad that would include Glassman as well as underlings such as himself. John didn't answer the question directly. His mind was rebelling. *Why am I putting my job in jeopardy by trying to convince the division what a good deal winning the ACE contract would be?* Meanwhile his mouth went on talking. "DAC has all but got this contract wrapped up if it comes in with a competitive price. The division needs this contract, and we can win it. We just have to have the guts to do what we have to do to win it."

Glassman wasn't buying what John's mouth was selling. He wanted to know exactly who would buy the other twenty-two computers.

John and Dan had anticipated Glassman's question and had prepared an analysis of the market potential for the DAC6G that justified the fifty-unit amortization. They didn't have the time or money to do a real analysis, so between them they wrote one, based on their collective knowledge, common sense, and what they thought would sell.

Dan distributed a copy of the analysis to Glassman and the rest of the staff. The top page of the analysis was a summary of the underlying details.

Dan took over the presentation to explain the analysis. Dan had the advantage of not being threatened by Glassman since he reported to a different management chain. Of course, during any management explosion there was always the danger of being hit by stray shrapnel.

The analysis summary provided an optimistic assessment of the DAC6G market potential. It described potential military and NASA applications and applications in the commercial financial market. It also pointed to a market of standalone computers in the hundred-thousand-dollar price range.

Glassman didn't appear to be hearing any of it. His voice became louder as he asked, "What in hell are you guys thinking? We don't have a budget for carrying any of the development cost on the books. Government

Systems isn't in that kind of business."

Dan didn't like the way the meeting was going. The DAC inside track on the procurement was about to be scuttled because of how the company was organized. He and John had worked hard and smart on this procurement. Okay, so maybe they sold something DAC didn't exactly have, but it wasn't something that couldn't be done. Okay, DAC needed to take some financial risk to ensure that it sewed up the procurement. *What else is new? It's that kind of business.*

Dan practiced remaining cool and calm during customer and management presentations regardless of the circumstances, He believed this was more effective than debating issues on the fly or displaying anger. However, in this meeting on this particular day, Dan lost his cool. "Excuse me," he said. "John and I have been busting our butts on this job, and we know we can win it. Because our nearly off-the-shelf computer can satisfy the ACE system requirement, we are in a favored position to win this program. If we include the full DAC6G development cost in our proposal, we lose that advantage. This is a big chunk of business for our division. It establishes DAC as a NASA supplier for a significant historical event. I know and everyone in this room knows this division is starving for new business, and this is a solution."

"Nearly off-the-shelf," Glassman huffed. "The numbers don't support that."

However, Dan's last argument touched Glassman in a vulnerable place. The ACE program would be a big chunk of business for the division, something needed and needed soon to replace programs being completed and phasing out. Winning would, as usual, entail financial and technical risks. These thoughts caused Glassman to dismiss the presentation team from the conference room, saying that he and his staff would discuss the proposal. They would call Dan and John back after they concluded the meeting.

Two hours later, Dan and John were called back into the conference room and told the decision had been made to approve the ACE proposal as prepared, on condition that DAC Defense Group Management would support the amortization of the DAC6G development cost and that marketing would commit to selling at least twenty-two DAC6Gs to other customers as a priority.

Getting the marketing commitment would not be a problem. They would commit to selling refrigerators to Eskimos if asked. Defense Group Management was a different matter. Permission was granted eventually, but Glassman was made aware that his job depended on the sale of fifty or more DAC6G computers. In turn, Glassman assured John Forsum that John's job depended on the sale of at least fifty or more DAC6G computers.

DAC Government Systems Division won the ACE computer system contract and proceeded to meet a very tight schedule. They had less than two years to deliver the prototype, serial zero, to the Cape early in 1964, where it would be used to verify computer programs. Many long days and nights and weekends were spent by DAC employees. They met the schedule. In July of 1964, the components of the first production ACE system were shipped to North American in Downey, California, where it was used to check out Apollo spacecraft. Thirteen additional ACE systems were supplied to NASA. Two of them went to Downey, three to the Grumman Bethpage plant to check out the moon lander, two to Houston, and six to the Cape.

While the DAC Government Division scrambled to fulfill the requirements of the ACE contract, Dan and John scrambled to fulfill the sale of an additional twenty-two DAC6G computers.

When the prototype ACE system was being installed early in 1964, they had not succeeded in inking a contract for a single DAC6G nor for a redundant system like the one used in the ACE system. John and Dan's efforts found they couldn't identify a single solid prospect for use an ACE-type system or for a stand-alone DAC6G computer in any military or NASA programs.

"Maybe we should have studied this a little before coming up with that fifty number," John suggested at one of their numerous come-to-Jesus meetings at a local bar near the DAC Washington office.

"Not necessarily," Dan replied. "We have to go with what we have, which is basically a pretty impressive commercial computer at a reasonable price with a lot of expansion and redundancy capability."

"And we have no contacts in the commercial world. DAC commercial doesn't want anything to do with it," John replied. "Maybe putting an IBM name plate on the DAC6G would help."

Although handicapped by their lack of commercial computer sales experience, John and Dan sold two ACE-type systems to a Wall Street financial firm that liked the reliability potential of the highly redundant system. However, the four DAC6Gs that were part of the systems fell far short of the twenty-two needed to satisfy the Defense Group Management requirement.

True to the stipulation that Glassman's job depended on the sale of at least fifty DAC6G computers by the end of the ACE program, he was invited to seek his opportunities at a place other than DAC. However, before Glassman had been given the opportunity to leave, he had provided the same opportunity to John Forsum. He would have done the same for Dan Daggart, but Dan reported to a different chain of command.

John soon found a similar position with another defense industry company in St. Louis, and he put DAC and the moon landing business behind him. At the same time, John resolved not to let a job that might not have his best interests in mind rule his life. His priority became family, which the family noticed and appreciated. He was home most evenings, became involved in the children's activities, and remembered birthdays and anniversaries.

On July 20, 1969, he was visiting a company on Long Island, New York. After an early afternoon meeting, he went to Kennedy Airport to catch a plane that would take him back to St. Louis. While walking through the airport lobby, he noticed people crowding around a TV monitor. It reminded him that the moon landing was to happen that day and here it was, pictures from the Eagle as the lunar lander settled down on the moon at the Tranquility Base. John felt a strong reaction to the scene on the TV monitor.

He was watching a historic moment in human experience in real time, and he had contributed to making that happen. Man had broken free of the earth's gravitational force and traveled into space to land on another celestial body. Ordinary people doing ordinary things working together can achieve extraordinary things. Such a thing had occurred to cause this moment that would never be forgotten by humankind.

All the ups and downs of that experience, even losing his job and having to move to different city, didn't matter at that moment.

Making the Numbers Work

Photograph is in the public domain

Making the Numbers Work

Jim Fowler settled down in his corner office with his first vending machine cup of coffee. The coffee was bad, but the only alternative was bringing a thermos. The corner office with a door represented a measure of his success as a longtime employee of the Data Action Corporation, commonly known as DAC. It had taken a while, over twenty years, to reach this position. Fowler started out as a mechanical design engineer and was eventually put in charge of all program management for all space systems programs. DAC had a reputation for highly reliable, lightweight, miniature yet capable computers for use in space by its government customers. Business had been good with President Reagan promoting his Star Wars missile defense system, but that could change; the Berlin Wall had come down a month previously.

A lot of pressure came with the job, and Jim attributed his overweight condition and loss of hair to the stress. He thought about exercising, maybe jogging. Trouble was he should lose some weight before he tried jogging. It was one of those chicken and egg things. There wasn't much that could be done about the expanding bald spot on the crown of his head. Combing what hair remained over the bald spot wasn't much of an improvement.

Despite the pressure, Jim liked his position as head of program management in space systems programs, with a staff of a half dozen working on proposals, program budgets, and scheduling, plus four program managers in charge of seven multimillion-dollar programs between them. He made more money and wielded more power than he ever could have as a design engineer, and he thought he had a talent for the job. He had a reputation as a good negotiator and was liked by the customers, prime contractors for the most part, like Lockheed and Boeing. He was also known as a demanding kick-ass type by his program managers and the department managers who supplied the engineers, technicians, assemblers, and support people who worked on the programs. Like most DAC managers, his background and training had been technical, not people oriented. As a result, the company largely depended on self-trained or gifts-from-God type of managers. Jim suspected he had been born with above-average management skills.

Jim's phone rang. He hesitated to answer it. It was likely Gerald Blackstone, director of the Government Systems Division, calling about an overrun on the Eagle One program that had shown up in the previous monthly financial report.

Gerald growled, "Good morning, Jim." Gerald's voice didn't sound like it was going to be a good morning.

Gerald continued. "Say, Jim… That Eagle One program is over budget, behind schedule. What are you doing to fix it?"

What Jim heard wasn't news to him and shouldn't be news to Gerald Blackstone. Alex Jorden, the program manager who prepared the Eagle One proposal, had instructed all the departments preparing the estimating to bid it skinny. The procurement would be fixed price and competitive. A potential for follow-on programs added value to the current procurement. The system would be used for satellite surveillance, something not likely to be cut from defense spending. Last, but not least, the division backlog had been shrinking, and without new business, there would be headcount reductions.

Alex Jorden had negotiated and cajoled the department managers to cut the bid to the bone, and then division management cut the already low-ball estimates by twenty percent. They were rolling the dice, betting that other division programs could make up any Eagle One losses so the division would be able to post an acceptable profit and level of business during the coming year. Now division management wanted to know why the program was running over budget. It was likely due in part to other programs not taking up the slack, and division profit margins were suffering. As a result, division management was under critical scrutiny by corporate management.

Jim hesitated. He didn't want to say what he was thinking, which was, *You dumbasses—what were you expecting?*

"Hello, anybody there?" Gerald prompted, after waiting a while for an answer.

Jim faked a small cough to let Gerald know he was still on the line. He was trying to think of ways to stall or dodge the question. No doubt Gerald Blackstone was under pressure from corporate to show a division year-end profit to be rolled into the corporate annual report. Jim began fabricating an answer to Gerald's question. "We are working the problem," he said without going into any detail. "I'll have a work-around plan on your desk Monday morning."

After discussing several issues with other programs, Gerald signed off, reminding Jim that he looked forward to seeing the work-around plan on Monday.

Jim rocked back in his desk chair after he hung up and stared at the ceiling. He didn't want to work this weekend on the "plan." For one, it seemed to be an exercise in futility, and two, he had better things planned for the weekend. He dialed Alex Jorden's office, located several doors down the hall. "Alex, you got a minute or an hour or so to talk about the Eagle One program?"

When Jim called, Alex Jorden, manager of the Eagle One program, was in the middle of preparing the customer's Eagle One monthly progress report. It was good timing for him. He grabbed a couple Eagle One binders and headed for Jim's office.

Alex had a boyish face and a full head of hair, which made him look young for a man about to turn fifty. A lot of activities with his two sons, nine and eleven, helped him stay in shape. Alex, like most managers in the company, had a technical background. Trained as an electrical engineer, he loved design and was good at it. Like many good design engineers, he had been rewarded with promotion to a manager of other engineers. It took Alex some time to realize he didn't like managing people, particularly egotistical engineers.

The problem with leaving management and going back to computer design was that technology evolved at a fast pace at the design level, and a person who was away from it for couple of years could become obsolete. Transistors were packaged individually in cans when he was designing; now they put thousands on a microchip. Instead of applying logic at the transistor level, they were doing it at the microchip level. Sure, he could do that, but it would be like starting over. He worked around the problem by going into program management, where he had to understand the nature of the technology changes but not the nitty gritty of implementing them. In program management, he didn't manage people, he managed things, like proposals, budgets, and schedules, and was the primary customer interface. He could handle that.

Jim waved Alex to a seat at a side table where they could spread out program data. "Here's the problem," Jim said as an introduction to what they had to accomplish today. "Division management wants to know why Eagle One is overrunning its budget. Apparently, they don't want us to tell them what they already know. We bought the program, an investment that will pay off someday in the murky future. Apparently corporate wants the contract to pay off today, to hell with the murky future. So, we have come up with a plan to show how we can make a profit from a contract we bought with a bid that we estimated at twenty percent under cost. How do we do that?"

Alex looked at Jim. "Are they serious?"

"We are supposed to come up with a work-around plan by Monday morning."

"We can give them the plan this afternoon," Alex replied. "It'll be a note that says it can't be done. We have technical problems we don't even know how to solve. A twenty percent overrun could be a low-ball estimate.

I'm hardly charging the program. I keep haggling with the department managers to keep the cost down. We have put as much pressure on the vendors as the law allows. Some of the vendors are betting on the follow-on, just like us."

Jim, who had been scanning a printout of charges on the Eagle One program, looked up. "That's interesting," he said.

"What's interesting?"

"Are you doing any work on Eagle One?" Jim replied. "Doesn't look like you are charging hardly any time to it.

Alex didn't like what Jim was implying. Mischarging on government contracts was a big no-no that could result in heavy penalties for the company and individuals. Alex managed two phases of the Eagle One program, one a fixed-price contract to develop a new computer and a related but separate cost-plus program to manufacture a dozen satellite computers of previous design for use in an NSA program. The production program had been negotiated a year earlier as a noncompetitive cost-plus contract. The government had little leverage, as no other suppliers had the technology or interest in competing for the business. As a result, DAC Space Systems loaded up the contract with costs, and the prime contractor was only able to negotiate out some of the most egregious charges. The result was a contract with a lot of padding, and Jim understood damn well what Alex was doing.

Alex replied to Jim's question. "You know time is charged to what you are working on—a program, a proposal, overhead, if you are on vacation or sick leave. That's what I do."

"Hey," Jim said, "it's no big deal. We all fudge project funds given opportunity and need. Maybe that's a solution, doing something like this on a bigger scale."

What Jim had just said scared Alex. "What are you saying?" Alex asked, hoping maybe he had misunderstood Jim.

"Well, you have two programs, one starving and the other fat. Same prime customer, same government agency—you just balance things out between the two of them."

Alex was aware of these kinds of shenanigans with cost-plus programs, where there were two contracts within the same program and two buckets of money. How you filled them didn't make much difference in the big picture, if they didn't overflow. But two programs, one cost-plus and the other fixed price, was a different story. People got fired, companies were fined and received black marks when those kinds of strategies were mixed. Alex had invested over twenty years in DAC and didn't want to risk it in order to make management happy. He pointed out these obvious problems to Jim.

Jim wasn't impressed. "There's more than one way to get fired," he replied. "The quickest way is to mismanage your programs. If you are given an impossible program to manage, you need to figure out how to manage it. I'm in the same line of fire as you are. I see a way to fix the problem so everyone will be happy and none the wiser."

Alex felt the pressure. Jim evaluated Alex's performance during annual reviews and made salary recommendations. Those evaluations went into his file and stayed there forever. A bad evaluation in his record could affect his future in DAC in a bad way. Besides, Alex was not sure how they could accomplish what Jim implied. How could they manage the timecard information? Alex couldn't think of a subtle way to ask, so he laid it out on the table. "How do you intend to modify the timecards?"

"Hey, Alex, as far as we are concerned, this conversation never took place. I expect you will work out the details. I don't want to know how it's done. We've accomplished what we needed to do today. You should get busy working on the plan. Complete it by Monday."

After leaving Jim's office, Alex felt a migraine coming on. He had been looking forward to a weekend of canoeing on a nearby river with his two sons. They planned to leave Saturday, camp overnight, and return Sunday evening. Now he had this problem hanging over his head, impossible to solve in any legitimate way.

Alex hadn't been asked if he agreed with the scheme Jim had come up with. Jim had decided what to do and told Alex to do it. That was Jim's style. So, Alex knew he would be in trouble with Jim if he didn't do as directed, and he would be in trouble with the customer if they found out what was going on. There were no good scenarios.

Alex decided he wouldn't let his work problems spoil the canoe trip with the boys, and they went as planned. The first day they headed down-river, the current helping them. They stopped often to observe the river's wildlife. They caught a couple nice walleyes that they roasted on a fire for a shore dinner that evening. They did some more fishing from shore that night and caught a few small sunfish that they returned to the river. They got into their sleeping bags early because they would be paddling upstream to return to their put-in spot the next day.

The following day, they didn't take many breaks because they were working against the current. The day was devoted to rowing. The boys took turns in the bow position. It was evening by the time they made it back and tied the canoe onto the car's luggage rack. Driving home, Alex was exhausted but felt that he had done a good day's work. The exhausted boys were soon sleeping in awkward positions in the car.

During the fun weekend with his boys, Alex had mentally worked out a plan to satisfy Jim's order to fix the Eagle One program. The scheme Alex concocted involved collecting timecards that were turned in by noon on Friday. He would then close his office door, select the cards to be modi-fied, and replace them with timecards he had altered. He would forge the employee's signature on the altered card by studying the genuine signature and duplicating it as best he could. He had tried to think of better ways but using white-out or cross-outs would be spotted.

Alex had also decided during the canoe trip that he would begin look-ing for a new job. The twenty-plus years he had invested in DAC had lost their importance after his meeting with Jim.

He discovered that the defense business job market had tightened. The USSR was collapsing, the Cold War ending, and technology people were exiting the defense business, crowding the rest of the technology world. Alex spent a month chasing leads, contacting every local business that might need his skills. He didn't want to move out of the area. He and his family had put down roots that would be hard to extract.

A month passed. The next Eagle One budget report showed remarkable improvement. Jim congratulated Alex on managing to improve the program's performance.

Alex began calling former associates who had left DAC recently to find out what they were doing and if they knew of any opportunities. He called Frank Dawkins, a sharper than average engineer who had been lured away from DAC by a startup. Alex learned that Frank had left the startup after three months.

"They didn't know what the hell they were doing," Frank said. "So, I decided to start my own company. Have you heard about a thing called the internet? It's starting to go commercial. I'm looking for C ++ coders. Know any?"

Alex said he didn't know C ++ but he was looking for work.

"What happened with DAC?" Frank asked.

"Short story," Alex replied, "I'm still working but looking to leave."

"Hell, Alex, you used to do FORTRAN. You can learn C++ like nothing. But you know I can't pay you like a program manager at DAC. You will be digging in the nitty gritty."

Frank described what they were doing with the internet, sounding more excited as he talked. The idea began to appeal to Alex. And he liked the nitty gritty. It wouldn't be hardware, but programming was the same kind of thing. "The idea is appealing," Alex admitted. "I can handle a pay cut as long as it doesn't last forever. How about some stock in your little enterprise in lieu of a big salary?"

Frank laughed. "All our professional people have gotten stock. Doesn't cost the bottom line anything, and we can all get rich together."

They agreed to meet the next day to talk some more. As a result, Alex signed on for a substantial cut in the salary he made at DAC and twenty thousand shares of the new company's stock.

The next morning Alex gave Jim the required two-week notice: he would be leaving the company. Jim looked shocked. "You can't do that!" he yelled. "You know damn well you can't do that."

"I did it," Alex admitted.

"Stay another year. You'll get the best raise you ever had."

"If you're worried about the timecards, I'll brief you on the process. I'll help you with it for the next two weeks."

"Dammit, you know I can't assign another manager to either program. I'll have to manage them myself. That's not going to work. I'll get you a promotion."

Alex had been focused on his own problems associated with leaving DAC and hadn't lost much sleep worrying about the problems he might be causing Jim. But being made aware of some of Jim's problems wasn't giving him any heartburn either. He made his best effort to sound sympathetic to Jim's concerns while suppressing a satisfied smile.

Alex soon became immersed in his work in Frank's new company, and it didn't take him long to realize the thing called the internet would be transforming the communications world. Frank's little company was growing as fast as it could hire engineers, programmers, and staff. The stock that had no value when Alex joined the company six months previously now traded on the local market at ten dollars a share.

Through contacts Alex maintained with former DAC associates, he learned the government was conducting an audit of the Eagle One program, an event that only occurred when something seriously caught the government's attention. A couple of months later, Alex had lunch with an engineer he had worked with at DAC. The engineer reported that Jim had suddenly left the company and the whole division was shaken up, with a half dozen directors being demoted or fired. He heard that Jim had been manipulating timecards. "Can you imagine anyone being so dumb?"

Alex shook his head. "Yeah, I can imagine it."

Risks and Rewards

Photo by author

Risks and Rewards

In a small fishing village on the shores of Manila Bay in the Philippines, halfway between Manila and Cavite, a young man named Modesto tossed and turned in his blanket on the floor of a Nipa hut. Beside him, the frequent stirrings of his wife betrayed her restlessness. Only their child in the near corner slept soundly. Finally, Modesto threw his blanket aside, picked his way to the doorway, and let his bare feet drop to the sand, still warm from the day's sun. From where he stood, he could see a large portion of Manila Bay. To his right and behind him, the bright lights of Manila made the sky luminous; before him the bay lay dark except for the dim lights of fishing boats that flickered and bobbed. Over to the left, a cluster of lights marked Cavite and the United States Naval Air Station at Sangley Point. The lights of Cavite also backlit an array of ship superstructures protruding from the water, the hulks of Japanese ships resting where they had been sunk during the big war that ended five years ago.

Modesto, small in stature, lean and muscular, had been a fisherman since he was old enough to pull nets and row a bonga boat. His jet-black hair and bright brown eyes were complemented by chocolate-colored skin that still had the smoothness of youth.

Tonight being Christmas Eve, he and Carlos and Chico were not fishing. Other than Christmas and Easter or during bad storms, they would normally be out in the bay fishing at this time of night. Their families depended on them to catch fish nearly every night. No fish meant there would be nothing to barter for rice, no pesos, no centavos, and no fresh fish for the fishermen's families to eat. Modesto was a good fisherman. There were very few days when there was no fish or rice to cook in his hut. There were usually enough pesos for at least the necessities and even for some extras, like during the fiesta and for Christmas and Easter.

However, the three fishermen would be taking the bonga boat out on Manila Bay this Christmas Eve—not to fish but on a special and unusual mission. Modesto left the hut and moved aimlessly along the beach. He recalled the events of the last three days that led to what he would be doing tonight.

Modesto and his two companions had been returning from an unsuccessful night of fishing in their bonga, a boat barely large enough for the three-man crew, their nets, and sometimes a good fish catch. They were tired and wet, aching from their night's labor. Intermittent rain, sometimes heavy, had combined with abnormally low temperatures to make it a bitter night. For their efforts and misery, a reward of only a half-dozen lapa-lapas lay on the bottom of the boat. They paddled toward shore in weary silence. As they rowed, they could make out the outlines of the hotels and casinos along Manila's Dewey Boulevard.

The crew sat in a row from front to back in the narrow boat. Chico, the youngest, held down the middle position. He looked small huddled under a bulky poncho. Chico, the son of Carlos, the oldest member of the three men, had only recently joined the crew. Chico had been a hut boy for marines at Sangley Point, a good-paying job. For reasons unknown to Modesto, Chico no longer worked at Sangley Point, and Carlos had added Chico to the crew.

Chico stopped paddling and broke the silence.

"The casinos are still lit up. As they sow, so shall they reap. That's what the church tells us. Well, we have worked all night and are so tired we can hardly get back to the beach. What have we reaped? Six little fish, not enough to eat, none to sell or trade. Did we sow the wrong thing? What do those rich ones in the casinos sow? They sow money. They don't have to sweat or sit in the cold rain. Money does their work."

Carlos sat in the back, the commanding position in the bonga. Wrinkled skin that had seen many fishing seasons covered his gaunt face. He laughed softly. "That was quite a speech from someone who's cold and tired. Remember, fishermen live from God's hand, and sometimes the hand is empty. That's the way it is."

Chico replied, "You been doing this too long and don't know any better."

"Maybe," Carlos answered, "but I know complaining doesn't help anything."

Modesto listened in silence. There were times he had felt the way Chico did, and sometimes still did, but he had a wife and child. He had to provide for them in the only way he knew how. Someday in the hereafter he would be on the same level as the good rich and above that of the not-so-good rich. Easier for a camel to pass through the eye of a needle than for rich men to get to heaven. That's what the good fathers said. Such thoughts made life a little more bearable at times.

Later that day, Modesto and Carlos were repairing one of the bonga boat's outriggers. Carlos owned the boat and, when the catch was successful, received an extra share of fish. Carlos had inherited the bonga, his most valuable possession, from his father. Frequent repairs kept it usable.

"I wonder where Chico is," Carlos mused. "He should be helping us."

Modesto pointed down the beach. "Speak of the devil. People with him. Who are they?"

Carlos looked where Modesto pointed. "Don't know."

Two strangers accompanied Chico. One, a gaunt, small-framed young man, was unremarkable except for deep-set eyes that glowered under heavy, dark brows. His dress, typical for men his age, consisted of loose-fitting gray pants, an untucked white shirt, and sandals. He could have been a Jeepney driver or a street vendor. The other man, dressed in a similar way, was taller, heavier, and had a round face with Asian eyes.

Chico introduced them. He gestured first toward the smaller man. "Pepe from Bulacan, and Wan from up north in Baguio City."

The two men surveyed the boat. The one named Wan walked around it and kicked the outrigger Modesto and Carlos had been working on.

"Looks small," he remarked.

Chico gave him a worried look. "It can haul a lot of weight."

Modesto wondered what they were talking about. What did it matter if the boat was small or could haul a lot of weight? It worked for what they used it for.

Carlos also looked puzzled.

The two strangers and Chico moved some distance away and talked among themselves. After a short time, they came back to where Carlos and Modesto had resumed work on the outrigger.

"Pepe and Wan would like to talk about a business deal," Chico announced.

Carlos looked skeptical. "Business deal? We are fishermen with no fish to barter or sell. What kind of business could you be talking about?"

Pepe asked, "Can you keep a secret?"

"Secret?" Carlos questioned.

"The business we are talking about depends on it."

Carlos answered, "You've been talking to Chico. He can tell you."

Pepe hesitated and studied Carlos. Then he began to speak. "Chico has told us that every night you and your crew fish Manila Bay, and that almost every night you go past Sangley Point. You may have noticed a Quonset hut that sits by itself right near the shore at the tip of the peninsula. Looks like an ordinary Quonset hut, but it's different. It's being used as an armory, and it's full of 30-caliber ammunition."

Pepe again hesitated, allowing time for this information to be fully absorbed.

Modesto felt a tightening in his stomach.

Pepe continued. "We will pay you and your crew a good amount of money to go in and get some of that ammunition."

Beads of sweat were forming on Modesto's forehead. He thought, *This man is loco*, but he held his tongue and waited for Carlos to speak.

Carlos smiled slightly. "This some kind of joke you and Chico thought up?"

Pepe didn't respond. "You will be able to make more money than you have ever seen before." As if to emphasize the point, he pulled up his shirt to reveal a money belt and a pistol stuck under his waistband. He pulled a packet of pesos in large denominations out of the money belt and fanned them slowly. "We will pay you one peso for every round that you bring out. Easy money, a lot of money."

The smile on Carlos's face disappeared, and the look of skepticism returned. "Easy? Why pay so much if it is easy?"

Skeptical or wary, Pepe knew he had the fisherman's attention. "You will be surprised at how lightly guarded the armory is." Pepe picked up a stick from the beach and drew a sketch in the sand of the peninsula that projected into Manila Bay, much of which was occupied by the Sangley Naval Air Station. Pepe added detail at the very tip of the peninsula to show the location of the Quonset hut being used as an armory.

"There is only one marine guarding this stretch of beach that runs from the brig on the east side of the peninsula to a point on the west side of the peninsula approximately a kilometer away. The route the marine walks is on a beach five to ten meters wide from the water's edge to an embankment three to four meters high. The Quonset we are interested in sits on top of this embankment at the tip of the peninsula. The closest thing to the Quonset armory, about a hundred meters away, are Quonset huts for housing navy and marine enlisted men."

Pepe drew the guard's route in the sand. "Besides the marine, there is a large searchlight mounted here on a water tower." He pointed to a spot near the center of the base. "This light sweeps the beach all around the base. You must have seen it when you were fishing. It makes a sweep about every fifteen minutes, then goes out until they are ready to make another sweep. Those are the things you worry about, the searchlight and the marine guard. Overpower the guard, avoid the light, and you can help yourself to as much ammunition as your boat can haul."

The fishermen were familiar with the navy base as seen from the bay and were able to follow Pepe's description easily. They were also familiar with the searchlight. They often saw it sweep around the base's periphery when they fished at night.

Modesto did not want to hear any more, but Carlos asked, "You sure there is only one marine?"

"One marine. Changes at midnight, next time at four."

"The armory is locked?"

"I would think so."

"We are supposed to figure out how to overpower the guard and get the ammunition out?"

"That's it."

"Why do you want that much ammunition?"

"Does it matter?"

"Are you a Huk?"

It didn't matter to Modesto if Pepe and Wan were Huks or not. He didn't want any part of this crazy idea, but he could see that Carlos was seriously considering Pepe's proposition. They had to be Hukbalahaps, the Huks, the Philippine communists. That was the only answer that made any sense to Modesto. They were the only ones who would need that much ammunition and had the means to pay that kind of money for it.

Modesto didn't know exactly what the Huks were trying to do, but he understood there was serious trouble between the Huks and the government in Manila. The Huks had been around for a long time. During the war they had fought the Japanese and were big heroes. Now they were fighting the government and weren't heroes anymore. It seemed like they wanted to fight whoever happened to be in power. Modesto didn't know if they were good or bad. Pepe looked like an ordinary Filipino, not like a revolutionary or communist, whatever they looked like. Not that it mattered much to Modesto. Modesto considered himself a pretty good Catholic. Carlos and Chico weren't, and they would admit that, and that was their business. If a person wanted to be a Huk, that was their business.

Apparently, Carlos had come to the same conclusion. He answered his own question. "I don't suppose it matters as long as we get paid."

"If you decide to do it, a thousand pesos up front, the balance when you deliver."

A thousand pesos! That was more money than Modesto had ever seen at one time.

Carlos didn't reveal any emotion or surprise. "Sounds crazy. We will think about it."

"Someone will do it," Pepe said. "We know Chico. That's why you are getting first chance."

Carlos replied, "We need a day to think about it."

"We'll be back tomorrow."

Carlos had fished Manila Bay for a living since he was able to do so. He had no hopes or plans to do anything else, and he had no hope of ever having more than a bare living as a fisherman. When Carlos became too old to fish, he hoped he would sit in the Nipa hut of his son Chico until the day they carried him out to the cemetery to lie beside the father he had cared for so many years before. It was not a great deal to anticipate but realistic and predictable. The wild scheme they were considering now was something else.

After Pepe and Wan left, the three fishermen discussed the proposition that had been presented to them. Carlos had done the talking when Pepe made his proposal, but now he wanted to know what Modesto thought of the idea.

Modesto had known Carlos since he was able to remember. Carlos's life was a model for Modesto's life. Modesto respected Carlos's judgment in most matters but had been surprised that Carlos seemed to be considering going forward with a raid on the armory on Sangley Point. Manila Bay fishermen considered Sangley Point off limits. Even fishing near it was questionable. To land on its beach and raid an armory seemed totally loco.

"It sounds crazy and dangerous," Modesto said in response to Carlos's question.

"Maybe," Carlos replied. He walked over to the outrigger he and Modesto had been repairing, studied it, then turned and spoke to Modesto and Chico. "We need more information before making a decision. Tonight, we will fish off Sangley Point near the armory and really study the layout. After that we will decide."

It was a little before midnight when they arrived at a position where they could observe the armory and the marine guard while they fished. Lights from the nearby enlisted men's hut area made the armory and guard path dimly visible.

At midnight they noted the changing of the guard and observed the marine on duty as he made his rounds. The marine moved back and forth along the beach between the brig and some point along the west side of the peninsula. As Pepe had said, it took the guard about fifteen minutes to walk from one end of the route to the other.

They had moderate success fishing and after a couple of hours had a sack filled with lapa-lapas.

At two a.m. Carlos suggested that they go onto the beach near the armory and check out the door lock.

"What! Why?" asked a surprised Modesto.

"We should know what kind of lock we have to break or open."

Chico agreed. "Let's see what it feels like to walk on the Sangley sand."

They decided that both Modesto and Chico would go to the armory to check the lock while Carlos stayed with the boat.

While they contemplated making the landing, they realized they would need to time their movements carefully. They wanted to go onto the beach once the guard had passed the armory and was heading away from it at the same time the light on the tower went dark. This combination did not come up regularly. The first time they considered going in, the tower light had gone out, but they weren't sure when the guard, who was out of sight on the west side of the peninsula, would reappear. The next time the light swept the beach, they saw that the guard was moving toward the armory from the east. They were concerned the light might come on again before he would be clear of the armory area on his way to the other side of the peninsula.

Finally, the light finished a sweep just as the guard was seen going toward the west end of his route. They pushed toward shore. Soon the bottom of the boat was scraping on the sand.

Modesto and Chico jumped out of the boat and ran toward the armory. It took only a few minutes for the two fishermen to reach the armory and determine that a padlock secured the armory door; a pry bar could be used to break the lock. They dashed back to the boat and rowed away from the shore toward relative safety.

The three stayed in their fishing location until the rising sun allowed them to observe the beach in more detail. It appeared that the path the guard walked was obscured from easy observation on the land side by the embankment that ran along the full length of the route. Their attention was drawn to two large tree trunks with roots attached that had washed up on the beach about a hundred meters to the west of the Quonset armory. Carlos suggested that would be a good place to hide while they waited for the right time to overpower the guard. They moved the bonga boat closer to shore and observed that the attached roots lifted the lower parts of the trunks off the ground far enough for a person to crawl beneath them. They all agreed that it looked like an ideal place to hide while waiting to overpower the guard.

Later that morning they returned to their home beach, tired from a full night of fishing and information gathering. They promised to get together that afternoon after they had rested to discuss the matter and make a decision.

Modesto tried to get some rest, but his mind continued to wrestle with the proposed raid. His first reaction had been to oppose the idea, to the point of defecting from the crew if Carlos and Chico wanted to do it. But as he became more familiar with what the raid would involve, his mind grew more at ease. A big factor in his thinking the previous night had been about their ability to get on and off the beach undetected. He contemplated the prize that would be theirs if they were successful. They could buy a large power bonga and have pesos to spare. They would be able to fish outside the bay and increase their chances of success. When Modesto finally drifted off to sleep, the contemplated prize loomed larger and the risk seemed to diminish.

When the three fishermen met that afternoon, Carlos again asked Modesto and Chico for their opinions.

Chico, of course, wanted to go.

Modesto had resolved his concerns. The prize seemed too large to pass up. He now supported going forward.

Carlos said he also favored proceeding.

They started to discuss the details. Anyone observing the three fishermen huddled on the sandy beach would have thought they were mending a net or visiting, certainly not planning a daring raid on a United States military installation.

They decided to stage the raid that night. The moon would be dark. Everything could be ready, and the sooner they put the plan into operation the less likely the wrong people would become aware of it. Also, early Christmas morning might find the security forces less alert than normal. They intended to beach the boat at about one o'clock in the morning, not too long after the midnight guard change. That would give them plenty of time before another guard change took place. Their only weapons would be machetes and iron pipes. The machetes were to be used only if necessary, although Chico wanted the machetes to be the first option. He argued, "A live marine can be dangerous, a dead one isn't. Besides, it takes more time to tie a man up than to cut his throat."

Modesto knew Chico had his own agenda with regards to Americans. His former girlfriend who now shared her place with a marine may have helped form his opinion. His abrupt departure from his Sangley Point job may have aggravated it.

"Taking some American ammunition is one thing. Killing an American is a whole different thing," Carlos declared. "We'll use machetes only if we have to."

Planning continued. Modesto and Chico would be landed on the beach and take cover under the tree trunks. Carlos would row the bonga back out into the bay. When an opportunity presented itself, Modesto and Chico would overpower the guard and break into the Quonset hut armory. They would remove as much ammunition as the bonga could haul and stack below the embankment where the Quonset was located to keep it out of the sight of the tower. They would use a flashlight to signal Carlos to return the boat to the beach when they were ready to load the ammunition. To Modesto, the plan seemed simple and doable.

Later in the day, Pepe and his partner returned and learned that the decision had been made to proceed; the raid would take place that night. Pepe seemed surprised that they were moving so soon, but he brought a thousand pesos in up-front money and they finalized the arrangements.

That night Modesto wandered along the beach, waiting for time to pass so he could join his companions and start on an adventure that would (pray to God, hail Mary) make them all rich. A few days ago, he wouldn't have dared hope for anything more than enough food to eat and the bare necessities for himself and his family. Now heady dreams filled his mind. He would be part owner of a big power bonga, a serious fisherman who went after the big catches outside the bay. He would have a Nipa hut with more than one room furnished with a bed and a cooking stove. He curled his toes in the sand. He might even buy a pair of shoes.

It was early, but Modesto turned and walked slowly toward the place where the bonga rested on the beach. When he arrived, he found Carlos sitting on an outrigger, silently contemplating the small waves splashing against the beach. Carlos looked up when Modesto approached. "Couldn't sleep? Me either. That happens often at my age."

Modesto squatted beside Carlos. Carlos continued. "Sometimes being old isn't so bad. I have less to lose." He hesitated, then apparently feeling a need to reassure Modesto, added, "Don't worry, it's going to work."

Modesto wanted to agree with him. "I wouldn't be doing it if I didn't believe it would work. Where is Chico?"

"It's still early. Chico will be here. He wouldn't miss this."

Chico finally showed up, yawning, at the agreed-upon time.

Modesto asked, "You have trouble sleeping?"

"No, why?"

Modesto laughed. "The resurrection wouldn't disturb you."

Carlos stood up and tugged on the boat. "Let's go," he said, and all hands joined in to launch the bonga on its special mission.

Each person assumed his position. Soon their rhythmic paddle strokes were moving the boat smoothly through the water, the bow making a luminous splash as it broke the flat surface of the bay.

Modesto mechanically dipped his paddle. The closer they came to the base, the more uneasy he felt. Was he a coward? Modesto had never done anything like this before. He had known danger when they had been caught in storms while fishing, but that was a normal part of a fisherman's life. This would be something different.

Carlos started talking about how this raid reminded him of ventures more dangerous and not as carefully planned during the big war. There were other differences. Those raids had been mainly for food because he and his family were starving. Sometimes he had picked up other things, too, but food had been the main thing. This raid was for money, enough money to change their lives. Another difference was that he disliked the Japanese. He didn't particularly dislike the Americans. Americans were overbearing, overpaid, oversexed, and drank too much, but Carlos believed that, overall, their intentions were good.

Modesto wanted to know if Carlos would feel guilty about stealing from the Americans.

"No," Carlos replied. "Americans have more wealth than the ocean has fish and taking some ammunition out of that hut won't hurt America any more than I hurt Manila Bay when I pull lapa-lapas out of it."

Modesto had considered the same thing. Was this really stealing? Would he be breaking any of God's laws? He concluded that some of the laws of men might be challenged, but not God's laws. The commandments as interpreted by Modesto pertained to individuals, to neighbors. Who did that ammunition really belong to? Maybe Filipinos had as much right to it as Americans.

Chico's voice broke into his thoughts. "Are you afraid, Modesto?"

Modesto thought, *Chico must sense my uneasiness.* "Maybe. I guess I am, but I will be glad when we get on shore."

Maybe he would be. His mind would be fully occupied, and he would not have time for imagined dangers. His thoughts of wealth and a new life from earlier in the evening were now crowded out by more urgent thoughts about the danger and what might go wrong. Sangley looked bigger and brighter than usual.

He turned to Chico and asked, "How about you?"

"Sure," Chico answered. "You can't be brave if you're not afraid, and I keep thinking the guard could be the one that's screwing my girlfriend."

Modesto laughed. "Used to be your girlfriend."

"That's what I mean."

"Don't do anything dumb with the guard."

"I know."

They reached the position off the point where they would wait for a chance to go in. Again, they watched the changing of the guard. They waited for an hour and then began looking for the right opportunity to land on the beach. They looked for the guard when the searchlight swept around the base perimeter. Twice they watched and did not see the guard when the searchlight swept the beach in front of them. Carlos leaned back against the stern of the boat. "No hurry. We will wait until we know where he is."

A while later the light flashed on again. This time it started at the far end of the base and moved toward the armory. As it swung around the peninsula, it caught the marine moving west away from the armory near the bend in the shoreline. As soon as the light went out, Carlos whispered, "Now!"

They rowed the bonga onto the beach. Modesto crossed himself, and he and Chico jumped out of the boat and found shelter under the large tree trunks. They carried iron pipes, machetes, and what they would need to bind and gag the guard.

Modesto knew that the marine would be armed with something better than an iron pipe. Successfully overpowering the guard had always been a concern, and the concern became magnified by the reality of their situation. Between the water and the tree trunks were over five meters of open beach, and the marine could be anywhere in that area when he passed them. What if the searchlight came on while they were overpowering him?

While Modesto contemplated these difficulties, he heard the guard approaching. He was walking slowly, quietly whistling some tune over and over. In the dim ambient light, Modesto observed that his carbine was slung over his shoulder and he wore a soft-billed cap. *Good, he's not wearing a helmet*, thought Modesto.

At that moment, the tower light snapped on and started sweeping the beach. The guard safely passed the tree trunks as he moved toward the armory.

"Damn," Chico whispered.

Soon after the light went out after its next sweep of the base, the marine guard could be seen returning from the direction of the armory, still whistling the same tune. He moved steadily toward the tree trunks where Modesto and Chico crouched.

When the marine reached the vicinity of the tree trunks, he paused, stopped whistling, and turned to look at the bright lights of Manila. Modesto and Chico made their move. The marine appeared startled by the noise Modesto and Chico made, but before he could react Chico swung his pipe and hit the marine in the back of the head. As the marine fell, Chico swung his pipe at the back of his skull again. "That's for good measure, Joe!" he hissed.

They dragged the limp marine into the shadow of the tree trunks, rolled him on his stomach, and worked feverishly to bind and gag him. Chico put the gag in the guard's mouth while Modesto pulled his arms behind him and began wrapping the rope around his wrists.

Chico stood up. "You can finish this. I'll open the armory."

Chico disappeared into the darkness as Modesto began to knot the wrist binding. Suddenly, the marine grunted, yanked his wrists loose, and rolled over, throwing Modesto off his back. Modesto landed near his machete when he fell to the ground. He grasped the handle with both his hands, raised it over his head, and brought the blade down with all his might on the neck of the struggling marine. The blade cut through flesh and cartilage, stopping only when it hit the vertebrae.

Modesto, still grasping the machete, stood up. He started toward the armory and then paused to pick up the carbine the marine had dropped on the beach.

Modesto found an upset Chico attempting to break the lock.

"The bar doesn't go through the eye of the padlock. How in hell are we going to break the lock if we can't get the pry bar in there?"

Modesto took the bar from Chico's hand, took aim, and brought it crashing down on the padlock. The padlock flew off, hitting Modesto in the leg on its way to the ground.

"Jesus Christ!" Chico exclaimed. "That should wake up the dead."

They groped their way inside the dark armory. They felt around and found boxes that must be ammunition cases. They started stacking the cases below the embankment where the Quonset was located. They had stacked four boxes when the light passed again.

While waiting for the light to fade, Chico asked if the guard was securely tied.

"He is secure," Modesto replied without any more detail.

The light passed, and they finished moving two more boxes, as many as they felt they could haul in the boat, and then waited for the light to go on and off again.

When the light went out the next time, they signaled Carlos. He brought the bonga onto the beach near the Quonset, and they started loading the ammunition boxes. Then, for some reason, the searchlight that had just passed a short time before came on again and swept along the beach toward them. Carlos urgently signaled for them to push off, but Modesto ran back to get the last box waiting in the sand. He gripped it firmly and started running back toward the bonga. Suddenly he was surrounded by blinding white light. He heard someone shout, "Halt! Halt!" But he kept running, until something hit him in the back and knocked him down. He tried to get up, but he didn't seem to have any strength in his arms and legs. Something under him felt warm. Blood, his blood.

He had the sensation that he was swimming underwater, swimming hard, but he was not moving.

He could hear far-off voices. "Did we get all of them?"

"The old man looks like he has had it. The young one is alive but scared as hell."

Modesto felt something on his neck. A hand? He heard a voice again. "A very weak pulse. Amazing what these Huks will do for their cause."

A dim light shone beneath the water. Modesto tried to swim toward it, but it kept getting dimmer and finally went out.

Cold War Short-Short Stories

Memphis, 1948

The bus rolls to a stop. I get on and sit right behind the driver. In two months, I will finish training to be an aviation electronics technician at the Memphis Navy Air Training Center. The bus moves through the training center as it picks up more passengers it will transport to Memphis. The bus is almost full when it reaches the training center main gate. A marine checks the passes, the bus driver stands, turns, and announces that all colored folks will now move to the back of the bus. I move to the back of the bus.

Korea, 1950

Damn, marine issue doesn't cut this cold. Must be below zero. Chinese everywhere, small arms fire from everywhere. I hunker down in my shallow hole. I'm shivering and sweating at the same time. My mind wanders—ponders my escape from that Dakota farm, a world to see, to experience. There is a scream, "Medic, medic!" A mortar round shakes my hole! I hold the M1 in my frozen hands. Do I dare show myself, fire this rifle at I know not what? Maybe milking cows wasn't all that bad.

War-Torn City Recovers, 1951

Two American marines, recovering from wounds inflicted in the war on the Korean Peninsula, wander around in a Tokyo market.

Tokyo bustles. Factories hum, making cigarette lighters out of GI-discarded beer cans, half-price Leica knockoffs, the world's finest china.

Two women stand out. One, a young woman, beautiful as many young Asian women are, a porcelain face with fine features, a tiny but full body. Beside her, an older version of herself. Both dressed stylishly in shades of blue.

The older woman approaches the marines. "You like daughter? Only 3,000 yen, all night."

Sangley Point, Naval Air Station, 1951

Tom, a marine a month out of boot camp, arrives at his duty station in the Philippines. That evening a corporal, a six-month Philippine veteran, persuades Tom to hit the beach.

Not far outside the base gate a toddler craps in the gutter. The corporal comments, "That's why the Orient stinks."

They stop at a bar where the beer is cold, the waitress seductive. The corporal introduces Tom. "Just arrived." he says.

"How you like Philippines?" the waitress asks Tom.

"It stinks."

She stomps off, muttering in Tagalog.

The corporal is impressed. "Takes talent to insult a whore."

A Different Perspective, 1951

I was a crewman on a navy patrol aircraft that was part of a group of four planes heading to the Far East for an extended tour. We stopped at Whidbey Island Naval Air Station near Seattle and spent a day practicing GCA, ground control approach, landings. That evening a fellow crewman and I dropped into the enlisted men's club for a beer. There seemed to be a lot of unaccompanied women in the club who were friendly. We talked to a couple of them. Yes, their husbands, members of a patrol squadron, had recently left for a six-month tour in the Far East and they were making the most of it. "Six months goes really fast."

Navy Patrol Plane, 1952

A navy patrol plane off Shanghai with fourteen men aboard is in trouble: one their two engines fails. Kadena Okinawa, their destination, is possible. It is night. A violent storm envelopes Kadena. Ground Control Approach is talking them in, shouts: *You're low, off to the right! Abort, abort!!* Impossible. The plane can only descend, not ascend. Somehow the plane bounces and stops on the runway. The emergency vehicles disperse, and the plane is towed to its parking pad.

A ground crew member sticks his head into a hatch. "Did ya bring any mail?" At that moment the crew chief realizes they have returned to the real world and answers, "Yeah, we got your mail."

About the Author

Alfred Wellnitz grew up in rural South Dakota, served in the United States Navy, and worked in technology as an electrical engineer. After retiring from engineering, he worked as a real estate agent before deciding to become an author at age seventy-three. He has since published three novels and numerous short stories. Alfred's first novel, *Finding the Way*, was awarded an Honorable Mention in the 13th *Writer's Digest* International Self-Published Book Awards, and *PushBack* was a finalist in the *Foreword Review's* Book of the Year Awards. Alfred now lives in Bloomington, Minnesota.

Acknowledgements

Talented people who contributed to the completion of this book are; Deanna Lackaff, editor and Sue Bonoft Durccharme, editor. Their work corrected errors, smoothed out the writing. Deborah Stocco, formatting and cover designer, provided the book it's professional appearance.

Support and encouragement were provided for my work for many years by the Pleasant Avenue writing group. Hosts are Michael Gilligan and Deanna Lackaff. Other members: Lore Roethke, Karen Anway, Dick Carlstrom, Daryl Anderson, Antonia Welsch, Joanne Esser.

Also by Alfred Wellnitz

Novels:

Finding the Way;
From Prussia to a Prairie Homestead

PushBack;
Deficit Triggers Hyperinflation, Terrorism

For the Cause;
The Cold War Turns Hot in Korea
and Why Young Men Went to War

www.ingramcontent.com/pod-product-compliance
Lightning Source LLC
Chambersburg PA
CBHW020822150626
46554CB00016B/623